TAMING RED RIDING HOOD

LIDIYA FOXGLOVE

Prologue

AGNAR LONGTOOTH

WANTED ALIVE
    By order of King Brennus
    Adult white wolf aged 30 or so years, originally of the Longtooth family, of the Stone Hollow clan
    Last seen where the river Ayl meets the sea, believed to be dangerous, particularly to the fair sex, and may be seen hunting the blue stag
    REWARD OFFERED: 50 Gold

I STOPPED dead in the center of the street. The parchment was fresh, pasted to the side of the tavern, right in the center of town.

The parchment must have come on one of the latest ships, bearing news and goods from the capital. I walked into the tavern, a place I rarely ventured. Men slid their eyes toward me, but in this peaceful town, no one gave me trouble, not even the drunks. Pennarick had welcomed me, as much as any human town could.

I walked up to the bar. "Mug of ale, please."

"I don't see much of you, Professor Wolf," the bartender said. He called me that, not that I was a real professor. I hadn't even studied at the academy. But Pennarick was somewhat of a backwater, if a wealthy one. "I suppose you're wondering about that sign. Have you seen the white wolf?"

I supposed I was rather transparent. "No…but I don't go into the woods much."

"Aye, you're a strange one. But that's all right. We don't mind strange here." The bartender half-spoke to one of the other men at the bar, who raised his mug to me with a chuckle.

"If he's a wolf, I'll believe it when I sees it," the man said, his words slurred but cheerful.

Most of the men in the bar were dockworkers and laborers, a little grubby—I could smell their sweat thick in the air —in shirtsleeves and patched trousers. I had come from giving an afternoon science lesson to little Robert Powers, who was too sick to attend school, and I was still carrying my bag of books and lesson plans, dressed in a dark gray wool frock coat, vest and cravat that was appropriately scholarly. God knows how I looked to them. I couldn't hide my golden eyes.

"What did this wolf do that King Brennus himself is after him? 'Dangerous to the fair sex'?"

"I'll tell ya what I heard." A sailor abandoned a half-hearted card game and sat down next to me. "And ya might want to lay low when ya hears it. They aren't thinking too kindly of wolves in elf country now."

"They never are," I said dryly. Pennarick was a human town, and somewhat isolated by forested hills, but we were still in the country of the wood elves.

"Brennus had brought his new bride back to his cabin retreat and these two wolves kidnapped her. Princess Bethany of Lainsland. She's a pretty one. They killed a few of his men, too. I heard he got to the princess in time before anything untoward happened—" He leered a bit, lingering on *untoward*. "But they say that the forest itself spoke to him—being an elf and all, you know—and told him there's a third brother and he's the worst of 'em all."

"And this brother...hunts the blue stag?"

"Aye. A big great white wolf, mean old bastard who hunts alone, with the sharpest teeth in the forest. I'd be careful if I were you."

"Yes..." I took a long drag of my drink. "It sounds as if I'd better."

Chapter One

FERSA

I DID NOT LIKE CARRIAGES. The last time I was in one, it was to take me away from my slaughtered family, and on to the damned work house. Today, the rattling and jolting of the wheels jangled my nerves and brought me back to that horrid time three years ago. The elves had killed my mother and the rest of my clan, sparing only the children. They swept in, their horses pounding through our camp, shooting arrows at the adults and snatching up the children. I was barely fifteen and scrawny, the oldest child they left alive. I had retched more than once in the carriage then.

It was my one way of rebelling against a horrifying situation. I couldn't fight back. I could just make myself unpleasant.

On this journey, I managed to keep down the contents of my stomach. I wanted to think I was stronger now than I was at fifteen. But I think the only thing that really made it better was that I was dressed as a fine lady now and I didn't want to soil my clothes or shame myself in front of my new family. I was going on to something better—hopefully.

I was scared out of my mind.

Father.

I had never known the man. He was a human, and my mother loved him, but they couldn't be together because she was of the wolvenfolk.

My opinion of him had never been very good. Who gave a damn if he was human and she was wolvenfolk? If he loved her, he should have found a way. But he didn't. She stayed with her clan and I never had a father. When I was in the work house, however, he was the only hope I could cling to. I knew he lived in Pennarick, a little town to the north, but I had never learned to write and in the work house I couldn't find anyone I could trust to send a message for me, not until Ellara came and helped me escape. She got a letter to Pennarick, and received a long letter back.

I had it tucked in my bag, although I couldn't read it. It smelled of perfume. My father had a new wife and she had written the letter back. It was friendly, I guess, but I didn't trust it. What lady wanted to take in her husband's half-wolf whelp? She was going to hate me, and I was going to hate her; I already knew that much. They already had other children, three boys ages five, six, and eight. Lord! I would have to keep my head down, that was for sure. Maybe he would like me a little, this unknown father of mine, Mr. Douglas Rafferty, but I had little hope for *Mrs.* Rafferty.

Ellara tried to give me a few "tips" before I left. *Try not to growl at anyone, or say 'fuck' or 'bloody' or 'shit' or anything else. Don't eat too fast or with your mouth open. Don't turn cartwheels unless you're alone!*

Well, no shit, Ellara. Easy for her to say. She might be

half-goblin but she was raised like a proper elven girl. I was raised like the animal I was.

My head raced over all this the whole journey until I thought I'd go bloody mad.

It took a number of days to get there, long days of jolting travel through the forest of Mardoon and sleeping in roadside inns, but before I was ready, the land opened up before me to the green fields surrounding the northern sea, and we passed handsome estates and tidy cottages and then came into the town of Pennarick itself. It was small compared to the elven capital I had just left, but prosperous because the original denizens were very skilled craftsman, and the town had ships in the harbor and macadam pavement and shops with glass windows and churches with tall spires. The trees had shed their leaves and the sky was gray, but the ladies strolling the streets wore brightly colored cloaks and fetching hats tilted above their curls. Mardoon was the territory of the wood elves, but Pennarick was largely a human settlement. A religious colony escaping persecution had settled there three centuries ago, and as they were peaceful people who imported goods around the realm and paid their taxes, the wood elf king was happy to leave them be.

Ellara told me all this before I left, and I think she meant it to make me feel better. *They sound like gentle, well-to-do people with generous hearts,* she said. *I think it sounds as ideal as you could hope for.*

I think I would have felt much better if my father was a rough, working man who cursed and spat and expressed affection with a rough clap on the back. I was used to hard people. I was none too gentle myself. *Gentle* people? What was I to do with them?

But since it had to be this way, I certainly was glad I had a private coach. It made me look like I was somebody. I can't lie and say I didn't care about being somebody, after all those years in the work house, getting sneered at by the bitches who ran the place. When I dared to dream, I thought about all the things my father might give me. Fancy hats, necklaces, silk stockings, chocolates, music boxes, tea cups, fans… In my head, I listed every nice thing I had ever heard of anyone owning, each one with a little punch of, *That'd show 'em*.

We pulled up to a grand house right in town, set back from the streets with a fancy rich-people garden in between the fence and the door, all symmetrical trimmed hedges. The house was painted gray-blue like the sky, and had two big bay windows jutting on either side of the grand, column-flanked entrance. As we approached, the door opened and people started coming out and standing on the steps, one after another. There was a lady in wide skirts and a man in a frock coat and three little boys, waving at our approach, lace ruffled sleeves fluttering. I guessed that the rest were servants. My gloves were shaking at this point. The coach trotted up to the entrance and the coachman opened the door and offered his hand.

"Miss Fersa," he said, announcing me. I felt flushed head to toe, and it didn't help that I had no real last name to announce. Wolvenfolk had clan designations rather than last names, and I suppose I couldn't claim to be a Rafferty yet.

The man and woman walked down the steps together. She was perhaps ten years older than me, petite and pretty in floral-printed silk. He was middle-aged and handsome with thick black hair just like my own. He bowed. She curtseyed.

I clutched my stomach as my body betrayed me with a wave of dizziness and nausea.

C'mon, you little whelp, don't get sick now. I forced a smile.

"Fersa, my dearest. Words can hardly express how glad I am to see you," the man said. "I'm not sure how much your mother told you about me…"

"Father," I said, the word very awkward in my mouth. I tried to curtsey myself. Was it a good curtsey? I couldn't have told you. I hadn't a bloody clue what a good curtsey looked like, but I wasn't clumsy, at least I could say that much.

"When you were born, I wanted to take you in," he said. "But she insisted on keeping you with her, and I realized a wolf clan might be a better place for a wolf girl. I would have sent you letters and gifts, but...there was no address. And I heard you never learned to read." I realized his tone actually sounded regretful. "I was always sending inquiries about the clan, trying to see how you fared. When I lost track of you, Katherine can tell you how distressed I was." He squeezed his wife's shoulder.

"Very distressed," she said earnestly.

"I've been trying to find you, these past years. As soon as I got your letter, well, I nearly wept with relief."

Wept? What kind of a man weeps over a thing like that?

"I want you to know that you're safe here. You will have everything you've ever needed and a great deal more. You're my daughter as much as the boys, here, are my sons." He patted the head of one of the unnaturally polite little creatures standing beside him. "You'll never have to work again, needless to say, and you will finally have a good education. Don't hesitate to tell me if anything distresses you in the least. I have a lot to make up for."

Katherine suddenly walked up to me and kissed my cheeks. "I'm so happy to finally meet you," she said. "You must be so tired and flustered, and worried as to whether you'd be welcomed here, and I want you to know that we all welcome you with all of our hearts."

I actually flinched back when she came at me, and then I felt more awkward and ashamed than ever.

I might've spent the past few years in a girl's body, but at heart, I felt like a wolf. I had a wolf's instincts. If someone came at my face, I felt threatened. In the work house, it was perfectly natural to feel threatened and follow animal instincts, because all of us were hardly treated better than animals to begin with. My pulse was racing with the tension of trying to behave like a lady.

"Th—thank you," I said.

Father put a hand on my shoulder and urged me up the stairs. "I want you to meet the boys," he said. "This is Thomas, the eldest; Francis; and the little one is John."

The boys were all perfectly tidy and well dressed and I couldn't help but feel sorry for them. I had spent my childhood running through the woods, sometimes wolf and sometimes girl, depending on what we wanted to do, and not a stitch of clothes on. They all looked at me curiously, John with a broad grin. I wasn't sure if I supposed to curtsey to children, so I just grinned back.

"Come in," Katherine said, taking my arm. "We have luncheon waiting for you. It's simple, cold cuts, I'm afraid, since we didn't know when you'd get in, but we'll have a hot meal tonight."

She led me through an entrance hall that was bright from tall windows, with a gold chandelier above my head and a staircase sweeping upstairs and polished wooden floors with carpets. I was glad I'd spent a few weeks in the Palace of Waterfalls with Ellara before I came here, or else I'd be too gobsmacked to speak.

Then again, I hadn't spoken much anyway.

"I'll take your cloak," one of the footmen offered. He pulled the ribbon at my chest loose before I said a word, and whisked the red wool away.

"A lovely cloak it is, too," Katherine said. "Did the elves give it to you?"

"Yes, madam." I stumbled on the word, unsure how to address her.

She laughed faintly but didn't correct me. Maybe she didn't know how I should address her either. "How kind of them. It's a very nice dress, too, but of course you shall have a whole new wardrobe, now that you're here."

I don't think my dress was really nice at all, compared to hers. Hers was a light, airy confection with a thin shawl, despite the chilly air, and no wonder, because the fires were blazing in the dining hall. And she obviously had a corset and layers of ruffled petticoats and all that rot, while I was just a drab little thing dressed in brown and green that fell straight on my body. Not that I wanted corsets and ruffled petticoats. I didn't. Not one bit. It looked very uncomfortable.

And yet, I also did. I wanted to fit in. I hadn't fit in since my mother died, and I ached for it beyond all reason.

In some ways, it was a lucky thing I'd spent time in the work house, where I had to learn to eat proper with a knife and fork, and that I'd had a little time in the Palace of Waterfalls to get used to fancy people. The dining room was filled with a table with seating for twelve, and already set with dishes of cold meats and cheeses and various salads and relishes. All the dishes and china were painted and edged in gold.

Father sat at the head of the table, and I was offered a place beside him, opposite Katherine, with the boys around us.

"I already have your tutors arranged," he said. "You'll begin tomorrow. We'll just ease into it with the basics of reading, writing, arithmetic, music and dance."

"Fersa can't read?" John asked. "But I can read. She's *big*."

"No one taught her to read," Katherine said, patting his head. "But I'm sure she'll be a quick study. You'll have to work hard to keep up with her."

Lord, I hoped so. That was the *basics*? "Just one person's going to teach me all that?"

Katherine looked at Father pointedly and he nodded faintly to her. "And diction," he added.

"Diction," I repeated. I didn't even know what that meant.

"How to speak like ladies do," Katherine said.

"Mr. Benton will be your music teacher, and Mr. Eldridge will be your dance teacher, and for speech, reading, and writing…we shall try this Mr. Arrowen." He shrugged.

"Try?" I asked. "What's wrong with Mr. Arrowen?"

"He's from away," he said. "And I'm not so sure about him. He just came to town recently and we don't know his family. I've never met the man. However, he was the best I could find on relatively short notice. And the Powers family speaks well of him."

"Aren't I 'from away'?" I asked.

Father grinned. "Well, we know *your* family. We'll keep an eye on Mr. Arrowen and if he doesn't suit we'll have to send for someone in the city."

"Why doesn't Fersa go to school with us?" Thomas asked.

"Fersa is too grown up to go to school," Katherine said. "You, young sir, have many years of study ahead of you. But Fersa has to know everything very quickly so that when she gets married, she won't be ignorant of the things a young woman should know."

"Is Fersa going to get married soon?"

"Who knows?" Katherine said. "Plenty of handsome young men around." She winked at me.

Oh, bloody hell. This was too much. Tutors and handsome young men. My cheeks warmed. No men at the work house. My dreams of what a man might do to me, if I could only get my hands on one, got quite intense at times…when the heat came on me. Sometimes I heard the alley cats yowling outside and I thought, *You and me both*.

I'll say one thing about the work house: it held the dregs,

and the haughty elven women who ran the place reminded us every day that we were the lesser races. There's a weird kind of pride that comes from that. I knew I wasn't any lesser than some stupid elf who ran a work house, and I was as good as any of the other girls there, too.

But what was I to the Rafferty family? I wasn't one of 'em, that was for sure. Too old to go to school, but too uneducated to be unleashed on society without lessons upon lessons on how to speak and move and read, something a kid like John could already do.

I couldn't tell if any of them liked me at all. I couldn't tell what they thought. They were all so nice to me, but underneath it all, I couldn't imagine they weren't frustrated and embarrassed by my wild presence intruding on their world of china and silk.

I tried not to speak, ashamed even of my accent, but they had no trouble talking, telling me all the things I would soon enjoy. Shopping for hats, the church concert, the oyster ball, to say nothing of the yuletide round of gaiety, as they put it. My eyes wandered to the windows, where I had a view outside of some rose bushes, a spot of green with some sort of game set up, and a wooden fence. Beyond that, I could see the roofs of another house next door and its out buildings.

I couldn't see any trees. I couldn't see the forest. I felt people pressing in all around me, not just in this room, but in the entire town.

There was nowhere I could be a wolf.

Nowhere I could be myself.

In the work house, they kept me in silver collar and cuffs, so I couldn't change if I wanted to, but I felt the ache. During the time of year when I felt the mating urge, it tormented me so I couldn't even sleep, but paced the floor until the other girls snapped at me.

Could I hold back the beast inside me? Could I be the lady they wanted me to be?

I can't imagine fitting in to this life. No matter how many lessons they shove down my throat.

Chapter Two

Fersa

"WE MUST DRESS you up and show you the town!" Katherine pronounced, as the servants were clearing away the dishes.

"I'm—I'm really quite tired," I said.

"Of course you are. But you don't want to go straight to bed after you've eaten. It will give you a vaporous gut."

I had no idea what the hell that meant, except that I wasn't getting any time alone.

"Come, come," she said. "I want to see what you think of the clothes I picked out for you."

"Katherine's always wanted a daughter," Father said.

"Although I'm afraid I'm not old enough to be your mother," Katherine said. "But I also wanted a sister. Aunts. Anything! My family is boys, boys, boys."

"Can I come see, Mama?" Francis asked.

"It's ladies' business, darling," Katherine said. "Best to keep it a mystery."

"You'll appreciate that when you're older," Father said,

offering his lap to Francis. "One minute your wife will be snoring in her nightgown and then in the morning she'll disappear and transform into a creature of enchantment, and you'll never get tired of it."

"*You're* the one who snores," Katherine protested, while Francis frowned.

"I'll take the fall, as a gentleman, but we know the truth," he said.

"I'm not gonna get married," Francis said. "I'm going to have a ship and it's going to be the biggest ship."

Katherine squawked out a laugh before covering her mouth. "Well, watch out, the ladies might like you all the more if you have the biggest ship."

I had to admit, my family had a good sense of humor and I sensed that they all genuinely liked each other. That was nice, in the sense that maybe they wouldn't take it too seriously when I made mistakes. On the other hand, I was not funny myself. Have you ever met an animal with a sense of humor? Wolvenfolk just aren't known for their wit.

Nor for their play acting. Dogs might be loyal, but they still didn't know how to pretend they were interested in striped damask. That was the situation I found myself in as Katherine led me up stairs to a dressing room, with a single gown hanging on the outer door of a wardrobe, and undergarments strewn on a plush chair nearby.

"Ellara said you had black hair and golden-brown eyes," Katherine said. "And you do—how striking! I thought blue might be a good color on you. I think I'm right." She took the dress and held it against me. "Oh, Fersa, the boys won't be able to take their eyes off you. More reasons to keep you shut up with your tutor a bit longer, eh? We must get to know you before you're snapped up! I can't wait for you to meet *Patrick* Rafferty. If I was a bit younger..."

"Er—who's he? An uncle?" I asked, completely flustered by her tone.

"A very *distant* cousin," she said, grinning. "There are, as they say, plenty of fish in the sea. Still, no one would complain if you stayed in the family. The Raffertys are one of the founding families of this town, and you can hardly throw a rock without hitting one."

She put her hands to her waist and glanced around like she'd forgotten what she was doing. "Oh, yes. Maybe you want to change into these fresh undergarments here, on your own, and I can help you tie your stays when you're ready. Have you ever worn stays before? You slouch a bit."

"No."

"Well, you'll get used to them soon enough."

Would I?

If anything was going to give me the bloody 'vaporous gut' it was these clothes. I traded my linen undergarment for a fresh one, and she laced the stays tight around me. They forced my body into an unnatural shape, the boning drawing my waist into an unyielding point at the bodice, and pushing my breasts upward. Beneath my petticoat she tied a little cage-like contraption made of fabric and wood that would hold my skirt out at the back and especially around the hips. The fabric of the dress was thick and heavy, settling around the undergarments. Over the dress I wore a short jacket with a jaunty little skirt at the back and tight sleeves with broad cuffs that she said was the latest fashion. "It will be cold outside," she commented. "This goes over your bodice." She held up a sheer bit of fabric and showed me how to criss-cross it over my breasts and pin it inside the bodice. "You might still want your cloak. Now, let me put your hair up."

She pinned my hair up into a coil at the back of my head and secured one of the jaunty little hats over it. A large blue plume fell forward into the edge of my line of sight.

"My, my," she said, stepping back to admire me. "You won't even need to open your mouth. You're a lovely, lovely girl and the men will go mad for you at the dances."

"What if I want to open my mouth?"

She laughed. "At your own risk, my dear. Especially with those sharp teeth of yours."

"This getup doesn't feel very sturdy." I gingerly ran my fingers along the hat and hairstyle, although my sleeves were strained to the limit reaching up that high. Between the sway of the caged contraption at my hips, the careful construct that my head had become, and how tight everything else was, I felt sure something was going to topple or snap.

"You're a lady now," she said. "You're not supposed to feel sturdy! You're supposed to beguile gentlemen with your delicacy. Nevertheless, it's somewhat of an illusion. It's all tougher than you expect."

"I'm—" I swallowed the words back. *I'm a wolf,* I wanted to say. *What the hell have you done to me?*

Katherine drew me toward the mirror at her bureau and looked at me, nervous, expectant, and hopeful, her frail hands clasped.

I looked at myself and was a little startled at the sight. Who was this girl? She *was* beautiful. I couldn't even connect her to myself. I patted my cheek like I was making sure this wasn't a dream. This girl belonged in the human world. This girl could have a human family...a husband...

I didn't know what to think.

"It's beautiful," I said, in barely more than a whisper.

I don't think even Ellara would have recognized me now. She told me not to curse or cartwheel; well, no worries about that. I would never cartwheel again in this getup.

Downstairs, Katherine showed me off to my father and the boys, and I could see relief in Father's eyes. "Fersa! I don't believe it! I always told your mother she'd clean up nicely. I wish she could see you now." *Now, you truly look like one of us. Yes, that's much better.* I swallowed back the lump in my throat, accepting the praise.

Coats and cloaks were gathered up for a stroll through town. They left the boys behind with their nurse. It was quite brisk out, and I was glad for my cloak because it covered some of my dress. I was so conscious of all the eyes on me: the new stranger. Father and Katherine introduced me to everyone we passed, neighbors and friends, young men who tipped their hats to me. I wasn't used to attention like this either.

Human. I'm half human. This is my father. I belong here as much as I belonged in the pack.

I kept telling myself that, but it was hard to believe. Everything here was so tame. Even their names. Miss Gray, Miss Woodson, Mr. Blair, Mr. Powers, each one like the next, so clean and polite. I knew I could never be myself. Fersa the Wolf would have to be buried so deep that she might as well be dead.

You're Fersa the Lady now, like it or not. But you're not trapped in the walls of the work house. You're taken care of, maybe even spoiled as days go by.

In a strange way, though, this wasn't the improvement I expected. The expectations were higher, and the attention already felt like too much. I tried to duck behind Katherine and Father whenever I could. As we walked, we ended up picking up a few extra Raffertys, some chattering old aunts and a middle-aged man smoking a pipe, Old Robert Rafferty. I would never remember all of their names!

I had managed to hang at the back of the entire crowd of Raffertys as they talked to a neighbor, when a man emerged from a tavern and bumped into me.

"Excuse *you*," I hissed.

"Well, maybe you shouldn't block——" He paused,

noticing the rest of the company, and his eyes softened. He swept off his hat. "I beg your pardon. You must be Douglas's girl." The rest of the family was moving down the sidewalk without me, and he said, "Don't get yourself lost now, eh, cousin?"

"Are you Patrick, then?" I asked, trying to sound a little miffed, but...lord, Katherine was right. Patrick Rafferty was a fine specimen of a man. He didn't look like a pampered gentleman. He was broad and strong, his shoulders straining his jacket, and he smelled like the woods, in a human sort of way.

"I never get lost," I said, which was true. Even now, I was sure I could've found my way back through the forest to my clan's territory.

"Well, then, your father might lose you." He put a hand on my back, and curse me, but his touch did feel nice. "Of course, you look like you might get lost on purpose, in which case it's not getting lost at all, is it?"

"Why would I want to get lost?" I had not really meant to get into a conversation with him, but here it was.

"You must have grown up out there," he said, gesturing into the distance. In the direction of the forest, although I couldn't see it from here—just buildings. "I'm sure you miss it."

"Has my father been talking about me?" I asked, tensing.

"He's been thrilled to have you with the family. Your father has a heart big enough to allow for just about anyone. Anyway, I would never have guessed you were wolfkin if I hadn't heard the story."

"Ah." Maybe I should take that as a compliment, but I couldn't.

He grinned. "We're coming up on the candy shop and if you stick with me, maybe I'll get you a welcome present."

"I don't need it," I said. "I'm full."

"I think you miss the point, Miss Fersa. Candy isn't meant to fill you up, now is it?"

My insides squirmed with a strange mixture of discomfort and desire. My moon cycles had barely begun when I lost my clan and was locked up in the work house. What would it feel like, to have his skin against mine, his strong body pinning mine down, our mouths mingling? How would I feel, to be with a human who could not change into anything, but was trapped in his skin forever? Would I feel more human too? Would I belong here?

My stepmother noticed us. "Ah, there's Patrick! What luck, I was just speaking of you. But now I've lost out on the fun of introducing the two of you."

"Sounds as if the luck is all mine," Patrick said. "It was nice to spend one shining moment with my cousin before all of the Rafferty clan had their opinion."

Now they were all laughing again, and once again, I hardly knew what to say. A poster caught my eye, tacked to a wooden building ahead. It had a picture of a white wolf on it.

"What is that?" I asked Patrick.

He read it to me:

WANTED ALIVE
  By order of King Brennus
  Adult white wolf aged 30 or so years...

"FIFTY GOLD," I said aloud in my shock as he read. *For one wolf?*

"Have you seen him?" Patrick asked.

"Of course not! Not like all wolfkin know each other. I en't seen another of my folk in...a long time." I bit my lip. "And white wolves are the rarest."

"'Haven't or 'have not', but never 'en't'," Katherine said gently, brushing my arm. "Try to mind your dialect, dearest. I don't want you to be teased."

"Oh. I'm sorry." I bit both my lips now, briefly, until the pain seemed to overwhelm my shame.

"No need to apologize. This is what Mr. Arrowen will help you with." She smiled again and shrugged at the poster. "I guess you haven't heard, then? Earlier in the autumn, Princess Bethany, King Brennus' new bride, was kidnapped by two of the wolvenfolk. Rogues from their tribe. They say she was unharmed, but think what could have happened!"

"I don't think some'll be convinced until that babe of hers is born without fur," one of the gossipy aunts interjected.

"You think a wolf would rape the princess? That sounds more like a story to stoke fear than anything," I said, bristling now for a different reason.

All the women looked at me in shock.

"Oh, my, we don't talk about things so openly," Katherine said.

"She was kidnapped, to be sure," the aunt said, shaking a finger at me. "It might be rare, but it does happen, and all the more reason the other Longtooth brother should be brought to justice."

"I heard the very forest itself demanded his head. He's been hunting the blue stags," Patrick said.

My father met my eyes. He looked uncomfortable. Then he said, "I would rather we didn't speak of these things around my daughter."

"We didn't mean—," Katherine started. "I mean, Fersa is just a girl, and half human. This man is a criminal."

"It's not an appropriate topic of conversation. Perhaps this wolf has truly done wrong, but we don't need to dwell on it ourselves, without knowing for sure. Gossip is not always correct."

I guessed he was thinking of Mother, and how the elves had slaughtered the clan. When elves or humans killed wolvenfolk, there was always some reason given that a wolf had killed or raped and the pack was a danger to civilized people. No trial was given. Wolvenfolk did not receive the benefit of the law. I gave him a wary smile of gratitude before he looked away.

Chapter Three

FERSA

WHEN I SLEPT, I dreamed of becoming a wolf, which was nothing new. In the work house, I always ran through the forests in my dreams—and often, I was running from something. Waking up in a cold sweat was common. But here, without my silver collar and cuffs, I woke up in my wolf form, with a wolf's senses. I felt the animal strength in my limbs, so different from my fragile human femininity. I was trapped in clothing and I growled with confusion. Where was I? My keen nose could trace the paths of the servants who tended to my room and I started to remember...

"*Mercy!*"

I heard a scream behind me and I violently shifted back, in such a panic that it felt a little like being born, forced from a place where I was warm and strong, into a cold and naked world.

My nightgown now hung around me with rips in it, and somehow the collar was shoved down my shoulders. I turned over, disoriented, and saw the maid cowering by the fire, her face pale, her chest heaving with panicked breaths.

"Ye's a wolf, missy," she said. Her accent was thick, much thicker than my own lapses into the dialect of my clan.

I gathered my wits, straightening out my nightgown, and scrambled out of bed toward her. She cowered even lower. "Oh, no, miss, please say somethin' so I knows ye's got your wits!"

"Oh, for fuck's sake," I whispered. "Look—I have my wits. I'm human. I won't hurt you." I spread my hands toward her. "Please. If you don't tell anyone about this I'll give you—chocolates." I had the candies Patrick had insisted on buying me yesterday. "I was having a dream, that's all. Now that I'm awake, it's all back to normal. Please—don't tell anyone."

She finally relaxed. "Ah...a dream. I see. Yes'm...I won't tell."

I handed her the chocolates. She shoved them in her apron pocket.

Someone knocked on the door. "Fersa?" Katherine called. "Are you all right in there?"

"It was me, ma'am," the maid said. "I seen a mouse."

"I chased it off," I called. "All's well."

"I see. That gave me a scare!" Katherine called. "Well, I'm going to ask the kitchen to make up some hot chocolate. It's cold this morning. You can have some too, Ina."

"Thank you very much, ma'am!" The maid glanced at me nervously as Katherine's footsteps disappeared. "But when ye turn wolf, d'ye have your wits about ye then?"

"I'm not turning into a wolf again," I said.

"But, supposing if ye did?"

"I've always got my wits."

In fact, I thought it was likely I would turn into a wolf again, in my sleep at the least. I had no control over it. I flexed my hands. They were stiff with cold but I hardly noticed. It had felt so good to wake up as a wolf, to feel the potential of strength and speed in my body and the way my senses came alive. I hadn't been able to change for those three years. Those years of my early womanhood were when wolvenfolk really learned to control their transformations. I had lost those years.

I was not at all fit for this world.

The maid, Ina, took some clean linen from the wardrobe. "If ye get dressed I can mend your nightgown before bed," she said.

"I could do that," I said. In the work house we did a lot of sewing.

"Ye might be busy with other things. I think Mrs. Rafferty is excited to have ye."

As she laced my stays she told me to hold the bed post.

"Why?" I asked.

"Ye don't want a wee tiny waist? All the ladies want a tiny waist. It's quite the competition."

"Well, then..." I was competitive, but this seemed an unpleasant competition. I dragged my fingernails along the polished wood, fighting off panic at my newfound prison as she yanked the laces tight. I shut my eyes and imagined my mother's voice. *Come now, Fersa, are ye a wolf or a mouse? What's to panic about? You have a new clan and they're taking good care of you.*

But I could only imagine what she might say. In fact, she might say the opposite, that I would never fit in here and shouldn't bother to try. I had never faced anything like this before, to be dressed by a maid in a ridiculous gown and sent to drink hot chocolate with a woman who expected a lot of me, in a prison of carpet and glass.

My father's house had a name: Meadow Lost Manor. I thought it was odd to name a house after something lost, but it seemed fitting. I had lost my meadows as well. As I walked into the breakfast room and saw him and Katherine and the boys sitting there quietly, drinking cocoa out of silver cups, it was so hard to imagine such a man crossing paths with a wolf woman, much less falling in love with her.

"You look lovely, Fersa. You wear gowns very well," Katherine said. "But you do have to watch the slouch."

"Aye, well, I've spent the last three years hunched over a needle and thread," I said, before I could help myself.

"The dance lessons will help," Father said. "It breaks my heart to think of you in that work house. Are they still operating? That woman there who wouldn't let you send a letter to us? I'd like to see her behind bars, I tell you what."

"She is behind bars," I said. "Ellara and Prince Ithrin took care of that."

"Good. I hope she rots there."

I saw a little of myself in his ferocious expression. "Father...can I ask you something?"

"Of course."

"How did you meet my mother?"

He glanced at Katherine and I held my ground. I probably shouldn't have asked, but didn't I deserve to have him speak of my mother? "Have you seen the painting of my grandfather in the great hall?" he asked. "You can hardly miss him. He looks like a mean man even on the canvas."

"I don't think so..."

"My father died when I was ten, so my grandfather raised me after that. If I can give him that much credit. He really was a bastard. Nothing I did, nothing my grandmother and mother did was ever good enough for him. He'd get on his drunken tirades and no one was safe. So when I was fifteen I decided to run off to the capital to find my own way in the world. I was a stupid young buck. Left my grandmother and mother at his mercy. The road seemed like no place for women."

"In these clothes, I guess not," I said.

He gave me a wry smile. "Believe me, I know just how you feel. At your age, I didn't want anything to do with all the rules of society. It felt like a prison. The inheritance just didn't seem worth it. I wanted to be free. A highwayman robbed me of all my money, and—well, long story short, I was penniless in the woods in the middle of Mardoon. That was when the wolves came upon me. One of them changed into a beautiful woman with eyes just like yours, and the minute I saw her I was half in love. I stayed with the clan for almost a year."

"Almost a *year*? Mother always said you spent some time, but I never realized it was that long."

"Yes, but..." He shrugged. "It really was stupid. Humans aren't meant to live with wolf clans. I felt like a dolt the whole time, not being able to transform, shivering in the cold without fur, never able to track well... The clan liked me at first because I could talk to other humans and deter them from going after the wolvenfolk, but before long, I was just a drag. And I got homesick for this world, for music, and tufted chairs, and cake." He laughed. "As I said, I wanted to bring you here at that time—you had just been born—but your mother said a wolf couldn't be happy in a town."

"But I hope that's not true!" Katherine said.

I stirred my hot chocolate with the delicate spoon and took a small sip. I don't know that I even *liked* chocolate. It tasted awfully strange. They damn sure didn't offer us chocolate in the work house. "So you came back and got married instead...," I said, unable to shake some betrayal.

"It was for the best," he said. "Your mother wanted me to start over and have a human life."

"I guess...she wouldn't come with you?" I asked. He had just said as much, but some part of me persisted in being angry at him for not saving her life. *If he really loved her, he would have saved her. He would have stayed close. He would have known where we were and, at least, saved me...*

He looked briefly lost for words. "No, Fersa. Surely you *know* your mother would never be happy here."

"But you think I can be?"

"You're *my* blood," he said. It almost seemed like a plea, deep down. "It might not be easy. But tell me, if anything troubles you. All of this ended up being my inheritance after all. I'm quite fortunate. I have more of God's gifts than the average man, and if I can't share them with my children, then what's it for? I think you have my rebellious nature, but in time, that will settle down and you'll see how good life is here."

I squirmed a little. *He didn't see her die,* I thought. *He wouldn't speak of 'God's gifts' if he'd seen her die.*

My life was decided for me now, that was clear. I wore what they wanted me to wear, I ate what was offered, I went where I was told to go. After breakfast, I was to meet with my first tutor. There I was, sitting anxiously on one of the tufted chairs Father said he missed, drawing anxious little breaths that made my bosom rise and fall beneath the demure-but-teasing scrap of thin fabric pinned over them. I was wearing a gown of cream silk with a print of violets and there was a line of bows down the front of the bodice and bows on my shoes as well. I wasn't sure where to put my feet or my hands. I felt so *displayed*. At least Mr. Arrowen, being a scholar of writing and figures, would probably be rather old.

"In here," I heard Katherine say, and she showed a man into the room.

Oh no. He wasn't old at all. I mean, I guess he wasn't young either. Maybe thirty or so. But that might have been the worst age possible. He was old enough that I felt girlish and idiotic, but young enough that he was still very fit and handsome and within the age of a suitor. And was he *ever* handsome. Tall, alert, with a thick chest suggesting a wolf's natural strength but also lithe grace in the way he moved. Maybe he was the dancing teacher and I'd gotten the schedule confused. But he was carrying a trunk that looked heavy as he put it down, like it held books.

Everything about him screamed at my deeper instincts.

"Fersa, dear, this is Mr. Arrowen," Katherine said, with a little twitch of her hand implying I should stand up and curtsey.

I did, as demurely as I possibly could. "Nice to meet you, Mr. Arrowen." I glanced up just in time to see the golden glow of his eyes.

He took a small step back, going stiff as a skeleton. "I think there has been a misunderstanding, Mrs. Rafferty," he said, in a voice that was so cultured I felt sure my eyes deceived me. He couldn't possibly have wolf eyes if he spoke like *that*.

"A misunderstanding?"

"I didn't realize...the young miss has strong wolvenfolk blood."

"Oh!" Katherine seemed to notice for the first time his golden eyes. "Oh, dear, I hadn't even noticed—your eyes. But —Mr. Arrowen, perhaps this is a happy coincidence! I think Miss Fersa might feel more comfortable around someone who shares the blood of her kin. And you know we don't judge here."

"No," Mr. Arrowen said shortly. "I can't. I'm not sure how to put this delicately." He picked up the trunk. "She is too young. Wolfkin girls have instincts that might be roused in the presence of someone else with wolf blood, entirely against her control. It would be completely inappropriate for me to take that risk."

The very word 'roused' emerging from his sharp canines,

teasingly revealed when he spoke, was doing things to me. This couldn't be a good sign.

If I had remained with a clan, I would have been mated by now. Wolf clans retained some human courtship rituals, such as dances, but generally we would have grown up together. As soon as we came of age, we would have paired off with very little in the way of preamble. Wolves knew very quickly who their mate should be; I think we could smell it and we were almost never wrong. If I had remained in the clan another year I would likely have been mated and pregnant before my sixteenth birthday. Rather than asking permission of our parents, the alpha bestowed his blessing on young couples, but it was almost unheard of for him to say no.

Humans thought this brutish, but to me it was the simple life I yearned for. Our roles were set and comfortable—my mate would have cared for me and our kits for the rest of my life.

I had no clan now. No alpha to ask for permission. I had not even seen another wolf in years. I assumed I would have to find a mate as humans do. As soon as I set eyes on this strange wolf, it was like coming home. *My own kind...*

"I see...," Katherine said. "But...there is no other tutor around..."

"Wait a minute!" I cried, snapping back to my senses. "You think I can't control myself as well as *you?*"

"I think I have a few years of control over you," he said. "I have worked very hard for my reputation and I won't risk it."

Whether it was over small waists or a disciplined attitude, I *was* competitive. I couldn't help it. The man had, perhaps unwittingly, thrown down a challenge. "Give me a chance," I said. "I know what you're talking about. Well then, when I go into heat, keep your distance. But I'm not going to throw myself at you, not now, or then neither!"

Katherine looked completely aghast. "I'm so sorry, Mr.

Arrowen. You see why she needs lesson in comportment! She's spent her whole life in the woods or the work house!"

"Aye, I see." He crossed his arms. "I didn't realize what I was getting myself into. I'll have to ask for more pay."

My eyes widened. "More pay!" He was audacious, just taking advantage of my family now. As if I was such a horror that he needed more money!

"I'm afraid that's what it will take to get me to accept this placement. It won't be easy. I'll be up late working on the lessons." He looked at me, his jaw clamping shut, a little muscle twitching there. I think he saw all the same things in me that I saw in him. To put it plain, it was the mating urge. I knew it from conversation, but I'd never felt it, because I'd never been around an adult wolf when I was old enough to feel such things.

Did this mean he was truly a suitable mate for me? Or had it just been too long since I'd seen another of my kind?

"Yes, of course," Katherine said. "Fersa, dear, please do try not to shout. It's no problem at all. Listen to everything Mr. Arrowen teaches you."

I shot him a glance and I already knew that there was only one thing I wanted to be taught, but then I remembered I had promised to control myself, and Father had such high hopes for me. "I won't let you down."

Chapter Four

FERSA

MR. ARROWEN OPENED HIS CASE, revealing a variety of books and papers. "I'm told you don't know how to read at all," he said, slipping on some reading glasses.

"No...not really." I added, in some defense, "A lot of the girls at the work house couldn't read anyhow."

"Your speech is definitely the first problem," he said. "It's somewhat of a hodge podge of accents, and none of it is proper. No girl of breeding should say 'anyhow', in any circumstance. And you have to enunciate. You have a habit of dropping and slurring your letters and even if we put aside the *choice* of words, that will help immensely. I gather that your father would like you to attend a ball soon so we have no choice but to work miracles."

Really? He would jump straight into lessons on 'diction' and 'comportment' without acknowledging this other feeling? It didn't make sense. Wolves didn't hide their nature like humans.

"So then what?" I said, unable to hold back a certain sullen reluctance to obey him. "Whaddya want me to do then?"

"*What* would *you* like me *to* do," he repeated, gesturing with a pencil. "Not, 'wot wouldjuh like me tuhdo'? And watch 'me' as well. Don't let it slip into a 'may' or 'my' sound. You want nice crisp vowels, musical cadence, *if* you want to be taken seriously by humans of breeding." He paused, raising a brow. "Do you?"

"Of course I do," I said, trying to watch my speech a little more.

"It isn't easy for wolfkin to assimilate. It takes a tremendous amount of will. You will have to fight against your instincts every moment."

"What about you? How much wolf blood do you have in you? Because it *looks* like a lot, but you act like it's none at all."

He exhaled with faint irritation. "This is why I didn't want to tutor a wolfkin girl," he said. "All that matters, as far as you are concerned, is that I have learned to assimilate."

"Can you shift?" I asked him.

"I *could*."

"Do you?"

He frowned at me and took out a board with the alphabet printed on it. "Do you know what this is?"

"The alphabet," I said. "I'm not stupid."

"I never said you were."

"Well, you surely do make it clear that you think it's better to be a human than a wolf."

"I never said that either. But you are *here*, aren't you? Making every appearance of a human lady? What is the point of doing a thing if not to do it right?"

"Aye, well, I don't have much choice, do I? This is my only kin now."

He paused. "Ah. I didn't realize. I thought you might have chosen to live with your father's kin."

I gave my head a small shake, avoiding the more painful reasons, and leaned forward a little. "You chose to live as a human, eh? Tell me why. Maybe it would be easier to put up with all this if I saw a reason for it, I mean, besides my family. They are kind and I don't want to be a disappointment, but lord, these clothes. These houses. These *manners*."

He handed me the intimidating slab of alphabet and then paused. "How about this, Miss Fersa? If you'll work hard with me this week, I'll tell you my story at the end of it."

"Clever man. You must know a girl loves a mystery." I jabbed my finger at the board. "Fine. But I don't make any promises that I'll be any good."

He seemed satisfied. I tried not to linger on his golden eyes. He might have tried to hide his nature under respectable clothes and a shave, but he couldn't hide from me. His eyes still held a hint of a feral nature, of something untamed and about to break loose. I couldn't help imagining that he would break loose for me. His hair was dark and thick, and I could imagine the texture under my fingers. I could imagine his fur too, rough and protective at the outer layer and soft as down underneath. He had long, slightly wild sideburns that added to the wolfish look. And he had a wolf's grace—stronger than Patrick, I thought, and faster. Nature gave wolves an advantage over humans even in human form— before you added cruel weapons to the mix, anyway.

I had succeeded in not lingering on his eyes, but I failed at everything else.

"Do you recognize any of the letters?" he asked.

His hands were stained with ink but otherwise very clean. I remembered he was, in this moment, no true wolf. He was the most un-wolflike creature you could imagine.

I pointed at 'F'. "I know my name starts with that one.

And I know the first four are A, B, C, D. Sometimes at the work house they labeled things as such."

"Well, you're only missing 'E' and you already have six letters," he said, like that was really something. "Can you write them out?"

"Maybe."

"Why don't you try and I'll write down some words that use only those six letters and we'll begin there."

I could tell this was going to be godawful boring.

It was even worse once we got going. Bad enough to learn all those letters, but he started going on about variations. Capitals, lower case, cursive. Why not just have one sort of letter and be done with it!

I was getting very fidgety before long. I nudged my feet out of my shoes. I wished I could feel grass under my feet. I wished I could run, wild and naked, drawing deep breaths of cold air into my lungs.

Snow started dancing past the window panes. My mind wandered away from the paper and I stood up to look out. It didn't snow that often in the work house. Wyndyr was farther south. Anyway, it wouldn't have been this beautiful at the work house. This reminded me of childhood snow. Fluffy flakes danced down from the gray sky and coated the garden outside. I pressed my fingers to the wavy glass.

"Miss Fersa?" His voice was sharp. "Where are you going?"

"I had to move."

"You could at least have communicated that fact. Are you cold?" he asked. "I should build up the fire."

"No, not cold. I just can't *think* anymore."

He looked at the clock on the mantle. It had only been an hour. He did build up the fire, anyway. I tried not to look at him lifting up a log and poking at the fire with tools; the sight was likely to stir even more urges than I already had.

Then he came up behind me; I watched his reflection approach.

"I know it's a lot to remember at first," he said.

"'A lot', aye, to say the bloody least. I'm not sure I can remember all that in a thousand years."

"An hour is quite a ways off from a thousand years," he said. "You have a quick mind. If I can learn this, you can. I was young once."

I snorted. "And you're so old now. You think I'm just a kid because I can't read?"

"I am an aging bachelor, at this point, and so I shall remain. You are...a young woman and I'm sure you will have many proper suitors," he said.

Well. That was a protest if I ever heard one. A tutor with wolvenfolk probably wasn't supposed to be good enough for Douglas Rafferty's daughter, no matter her own personal circumstances.

"Mr. Arrowen, I bet right now you're not really thinking about the alphabet."

He didn't take the bait. "If you need a break, take a short walk and return. I'll prepare a mathematics lesson," he said.

What was *wrong* with him? Wolves didn't court and get married. Wolves acted on their instincts of attraction, and if he and I had met as wolves, we wouldn't be dancing around.

I rolled my eyes at the window, but I was quick to leave. I wrapped my cloak around me and walked the garden, glancing occasionally at the window to see if he was watching me.

He wasn't.

The horrible lessons went on until lunch, at which time I met my other tutors for the music and dance lessons. Dance was the best of them. I wasn't great at following instructions, but at least I could move my feet. The music was just as strange to me as letters or arithmetic, but it was also so beautiful that I kept forgetting to breathe.

If I wasn't getting my head stuffed with lessons, I was expected to learn how to be a proper girl by example. Sometimes Katherine had callers and sometimes she went calling herself, and either way, she wanted to introduce me and make me a part of town life. These strange ladies talked of town events, weather, distant wars, what the ships had brought in, and countless other things, often while knitting or embroidering. They treated me with kind, polite curiosity.

I wanted to be free. All those years in the work house, I dreamed of being free. I still couldn't have that. Father said I couldn't go out without a chaperone, except in the garden, which was too small to do more than pace like a captive.

Just like I used to do on the bare work house lawn.

Patrick stopped by one afternoon to ask if I would like to take a walk. Apparently, that was how it went. Ladies waited for men to air them out.

But he was handsome, and less complicated than Mr. Arrowen, I must say. He was less a wolf, more of a friendly hunting dog. He apologized for being sweaty. "I was practicing my archery," he said. "I know, even in the snow."

"I don't think it's strange. I like being outside. I'm heartier than I look in these clothes," I said.

"Is it strange for you, getting used to town life?" he asked.

"Aye, to say the least! The clothes are so impractical, but the food is very good and that makes up for a lot."

"It does. Have people been welcoming?"

"Yes... I mean, mostly. Everyone's been calling me 'Little Red Hood' or some variation. I think they don't like my name. It's a wolf name."

He bristled, one hand curling into a loose fist. "Who's insulting you?"

"Not insulting me." I lightly touched his arm, grinning. Aye, that was the proper attitude for a man. "No need to beat anyone up on my behalf. They aren't cruel. I'm actually surprised. I thought a girl of my kind would face more judgment."

"I think it's cute," he said. "Little Red Hood."

"Aye, but still..." I trailed off. No, it was no use complaining. "Never mind."

"You can talk to me," he said.

"Well...I shouldn't say anything. I just feel like...an outsider. Katherine says something every time I make a misstep. 'Fersa, dear...' Sometimes I actually wish someone would take a *real* shot at me so I could fight back. Oh, that sounds ridiculous."

"Not at all. You're a fighter, aren't you?"

"Mm..."

"Fighters like the fight, don't they? That's how you get it all out of your head, in the end."

"That's it. That's exactly it."

I had never felt so confused. I wasn't sure if I hated my new life, or if I was absolutely desperate to shape myself to fit...if I enjoyed taking walks with Patrick Rafferty, or chafed at the fact that I had to wait for him to take me out.

"Still struggling with the reading?" Father asked at dinner. "You'll get there. I can only imagine trying to teach your mother to read! She wasn't patient with such things."

"Fersa definitely has some patience," Katherine said. "You should have seen the little squirrel she embroidered the other day. It was so sweet with its long ears!"

"I remember those sorts of squirrels," Father said. "We don't have them in Pennarick."

"I'm glad I have some useful talent. Mr. Benton tried to teach me to sing today," I said. "But he says I howl."

The whole family laughed at that. "Mama, I can howl!"

John cried; the youngest boy was definitely the kid who wanted all the attention. "Arooooo!"

"Not at the table, dear."

But these perfectly human moments were nothing compared to the wild desire that haunted me at night. Nearly every morning, I woke up a wolf. I had to start sleeping in the nude so I wouldn't damage my nightgown. Only the maid ever saw me, but it was only a matter of time before Katherine found out. I wondered what she would say. Maybe nothing, but I was still ashamed that I couldn't control myself.

On Friday morning after I had changed back into a girl and put on my nightgown, waiting for Ina to dress me for another tedious day, I heard the boys outside my door.

"I dare you," I heard Thomas whisper.

"Mmm..."

"You scared?"

"No..."

"You scared of wolves? She might turn into a wolf if we scare her."

"I'm not scared of wolves! I wouldn't be scared if Fersa was a wolf!" That was John. "I wish she *would* turn into one."

"She's just a normal girl," Francis said. "Boring. She'll be mad and Father will punish us for bothering her."

I paused at washing my face. Normal? Boring? I couldn't stand *that*.

I rushed to the door and flung it open, hunching down to their level. "Raaawr!"

All three of them screamed and jumped back. Then they started laughing.

"Did you hear us?" Thomas asked, clearly concerned.

"Just a bit. Just that I'm boring. *I'm* not boring. This *world* is boring, did you ever think of that? How did you escape this morning?"

Thomas laughed. "We got dressed quickly this morning so we could play."

"Play, huh?" I turned a cartwheel down the hall. This seemed like one moment where I could be myself, entertaining little boys before the daily schedule began.

"Teach me to do that!" John gasped. "Can you turn into a wolf?"

"That's not proper!" Francis hissed. "She can't do that!"

I laughed. "Now that you've asked, I don't know if I can help it. You just have to promise me one thing."

"What?" John asked, his eyes growing wide and excited. I hadn't seen the boys light up like this all week. Usually they were neatly handling silverware and being reprimanded for being too boisterous. They only got to be really noisy in the afternoon when they got home from school and their nurse took them outside for a little while. That was usually during my music lesson and it always made me want to run outside with them.

"One, that you won't tell anyone. It'a a secret, all right?"

They all nodded eagerly. "Yes, yes."

"And two, that when I go back into my room in wolf form, you'll shut the door behind me so I can change into a girl again and get dressed."

They giggled. "Okay."

I dropped down, letting myself fall into an easy shift. It was the first time I'd changed on purpose, and it felt wonderful to allow my body to do what it wanted to do. I tried my best to shift out of my clothes, pulling my arms out of the sleeves just before the transformation overcame me, but I still felt the fabric rip a little around my chest. I backed out of my nightgown, shaking it off of my fur.

The boys were gasping and clutching each other's hands. I ran a circle around them and licked John's face, relishing my senses. I could smell and taste them acutely, and it gave me a better sense of them in ways I could not explain in human language. My wolf self had instincts that I could only grasp at as a girl.

Now, I wanted to make them grin wider and never think of me as boring again. I nipped the collar of John's pajamas and tugged him toward my back.

"I think she's letting you have a ride!" Francis said.

I stood still and let the smallest boy climb onto me, clutching my fur. I snorted. *Hang on if you know what's good for you.* I ran down the hall. John let out a squeal of pure excitement, his arms tight around my neck. He started slipping off when I turned to run back. I tried to slow down but he fell off into a laughing mess of rumpled hair and clothes.

"Can I? Am I too big?" Francis asked.

Thomas was probably too big. I thought I could handle Francis. I let him clamber on, and I loped by John and clamped my teeth on the hem of his shirt, nudging him up.

Wolves were never too old to play. Good for the soul, Mother said. Chasing and good-natured scuffling kept our instincts keen. My wolf self had almost forgotten where I was, and that role of polite, well-dressed girl I had been forced to play.

That is, until I heard male voices approach quickly down the hall and my father's voice call sharply, "Fersa!"

I looked up. He was walking with Mr. Arrowen. He looked stunned. I froze in complete horror.

Father ran toward us. "None of you are hurt, are you?"

The spell had been broken. I rushed into my bedroom. No one closed the door, so I scurried under the bed and changed back there where no one could see me. "Close the door!" I barked. "Of course none of them are hurt! I was just playing!"

Father shut the door.

I was there among a few dust motes, breathing hard until

I sneezed. My cheeks were burning. I was ashamed at being caught, annoyed that he would think I might hurt anyone, and—devastated. I should have known better. I had broken the rules.

"Fersa," Father said, tapping on the door now. "I know you wouldn't hurt them on purpose. Wolves can get a little rough, that's all."

I crawled out, my limbs a bit shaky, and struggled to stuff my head and arms in the right holes of the nightgown. I opened the door. "We were having fun," I said. "It's early. I thought it would be all right. Why is Mr. Arrowen here?"

"I told him he could borrow some books," Father said. "I have so many, but not much time for reading. He's an interesting fellow. We just got to chatting a bit." He shrugged and then put a heavy hand on my shoulder. "Boys, I think it's past time you get to breakfast. Mr. Arrowen, you can wait in the library."

The boys were hesitant as they headed off down the hall. I think they were worried they'd gotten me into trouble. *As well they should be...* They sure had yelled enough. But in the end, it was my fault. I tried to smile at them before they were gone.

Mr. Arrowen tipped his hat, but his eyes briefly bored into me before he walked away.

"You see," Father said, "I truly do understand—as well as a human can, I suppose—what you're going through now. That's what we were just talking about, actually, the vast difference between living with a wolf clan and living in a town like this. I'm not sure how I can make it easier for you. I could let you take things more slowly but what would that accomplish? I can't return you to the woods, to your clan. I can't bring your mother back... I would make it harder for you to be a part of things. I want to give you a home but I also have to make sure that the home I can offer will accept you as a part of it. I don't have control over that."

"I don't know the answer either. And this is so much better than the work house. I don't want to seem an ungrateful wretch. It's just, I'm not sure my brain's made for letters and sums and sheets of music... Mr. Arrowen seems to think I'm talking myself into failure. Maybe. I did have to sit and behave at the work house, but I didn't have to *think*."

Father smiled. "Maybe I'm trying too hard to protect you from 'talk'. Nevertheless...do try. I've already had to clean up after myself. Still, I guess there's no harm in letting you play with the boys."

"They thought I was boring."

"We don't want that, do we?"

"No." I returned his smile, and I thought everything was all right. But at breakfast, Katherine was a little tense. Before I started my lessons, she said, "I heard what happened. I hope everything's all right."

I never knew what to say. What did that even *mean*? I couldn't read her. Humans said one thing when they meant another. "'Course it is," I said. "The boys wanted to see it, that's all."

"Mm. I'm not sure we should encourage them to act like animals any more than they do... And your tutor saw you!"

"Well, how was I supposed to know he'd come early? And I don't think the boys act like animals. They seem more like angels to me." I refrained from saying, *far too* much *like angels*.

"As long as you're in control."

Now I was starting to think she suspected what was happening to me in the mornings. Servants probably weren't that good at keeping secrets. "I am," I said. "You see me often enough. I'm in control all day long!" That was true. I was in control during the day. I could hardly help what happened as I dreamed.

"Well, Mr. Arrowen *did* say you've been making progress with your reading and writing. He's giving you an astronomy lesson this evening."

"Astronomy?"

She paused. "I thought it was an unusual request. If he ever behaves inappropriately around you, tell me straight-away. He is your tutor, but nothing more."

My brow furrowed. "To tell you the truth, he's quite a stick."

Katherine's lips quirked. "Good. He should be."

Chapter Five

❦

Agnar

A man—or a wolf who wants to live as a man does—has to make a living somehow. I should never have agreed to tutor a girl with sharp teeth and wild eyes, but I could hardly refuse the wage.

I knew how to teach letters and numbers. But teaching a wolfkin girl how to be human was the last thing I should have been teaching. I knew how hard a thing it was to learn—and that, when I had wanted it. As far as I could tell, she didn't want it much.

Every day, she could hardly make it through an hour of instruction without fidgeting. She would abruptly get up and spring to the window if she saw a bird or falling snow. And when I tried to call her attention back to me and my lessons, I knew it was a losing battle. She would give me a withering look.

"Come on, we need to stretch our legs, don't we?"

I had to clench my nails against my palm not to lose my mind. Watching her fluid movements, I could just imagine running in the forest, the wild smell of it—and her. My imagination ran to the same places hers did. I could see it in her eyes, a briefly shared dream. And with every day, that dream was growing more inappropriate.

The dream was far too dangerous for me to pursue. And I could practically feel my intelligence bleeding out of my head. My cock didn't care about letters. It throbbed in my trousers when she moved the right way, and I caught a good look at her breasts, or when she wet her lips with her tongue. It was bad enough to be around human girls, but they didn't do this to me. The urge to mate, to have kits with this lovely young wolfkin girl, was crumbling away at the resolve I had built up over fifteen years.

Quit. Quit now before you lose everything, the voice of sense prodded me.

But I wasn't going to quit. I already knew that. The moment I asked for more money, I had doomed myself, hadn't I?

"Sit down," I said, trying to sound cool and commanding.

"Oof. You're impossible." She finally slumped back into her seat but her eyes were still pointed toward the window.

"Just a little more, Miss Fersa. You can manage this much."

"I'm falling asleeeeep." She flopped her head onto the table and then straightened up again. "Ouch. These clothes pinch me when I slump!"

"I think that's the idea."

"Damnable torture chamber," she muttered.

"The lessons will be more interesting when you can read. We can move on to other subjects. Have you seen your father's library? It's a wealth of riches."

"I'll never be able to read! It all looks like gibberish. I don't even want to read. I've never needed it before and I'm *fine*. Plenty of people can't read."

"People who can't afford an education can't read. Do you know what a gift it is, to be able to have an education?"

She rolled her eyes. "No, but you're going to tell me, I have a feeling."

I tapped a pencil against the table. I'd had hardheaded students before. Usually the younger children. Never...

My eyes drifted to the perfect, round breasts that her dress so helpfully emphasized, partially shrouded by a thin scrap of cloth. One flick of my finger would tear that cloth away. I could only imagine the soft curves of the body underneath.

I shut my eyes and kneaded the bridge of my nose, mentally naming the planets.

I heard Fersa writing something now. The barest tip of her tongue poked out of her teeth as she carefully wrote *C...A...*

"That's better," I said. "Very nice."

D, she wrote, with a little flourish.

"Did I get it right? C-A-D, *cad*?"

"Are you trying to send me a message?"

"You think? Of course, you're not really a cad. More of a bore."

I didn't show any sign of outward irritation. "And how do you think that is spelled?"

"I haven't got any idea!"

"What do you think the first letter is?" I asked patiently. "You should be able to figure out that much."

She glared. "B."

"And then?"

"A?"

"Try again."

She clutched her head. "It's too much!"

"Too much? Just think. What are the vowels?"

"A...e...o...i...? Oh, rot! They all make different sounds depending, and they have different combinations that are completely confusing, and—and I think you're a lousy teacher! Pushing me too hard!" She got to her feet, pacing. "I can't think like this and I don't know how you can either! What's the point?"

"It's a good question..." Tonight, I would try my best to explain it to her, but I wondered if I could. When I was young, the desire to know more felt like an unhealthy addiction. In the end, I wasn't sure it had improved my life at all. As a child, I was happy. It all began to go downhill for me on the day I saw that the telescope. I had lost everything thanks to that telescope. Maybe I wasn't doing her any favors.

"Wolves might be happier than humans," I admitted. "The more you learn, the more you question."

"I think so," she said. "And why question? Pretty soon I'll be moping around thinking about death and god and things like that like Janey."

"Who's Janey?"

"A girl I used to work with." She tilted her head.

"Would you like our lessons to end?"

"Not like I have a choice."

"Why not? I'm just a hired tutor. I have only been in Pennarick for a few months and I haven't exactly befriended the town gossips. I take it you are unable to return to your clan..."

She paused. "The elves killed my clan. They thought we were menacing the town. They let the kids live. I was about fifteen. I was the oldest one who got to live and they sent me to a work house, making sails for their ships, things like that, until I finally managed to get a letter to my father....years later." She looked at me with her face pinched and stubborn. "But I'm tough. I don't want to talk and get weepy about it."

I was briefly rendered speechless, but I quickly nodded.

"I'm smart in the ways that matter," she added. "You remind me of those elves in Wyndyr. All high and mighty."

"I am not 'high and mighty'. I think you'll find that most tutors are somewhat strict. It's my job."

"Is all this just so I can marry some stupid man? Can't my servants do sums for me?"

"If you're going to marry a stupid man, you should *definitely* know these things. Do you trust your servants as much as you trust your own self?"

She definitely understood that perspective. I didn't expect that she was a very trusting girl.

"I'm not sure what to tell you," I said. "If you want me to say that the life of wolvenfolk is superior to this...well, maybe it is. But it's not a life I can return to, personally. If it's a life you can return to, then maybe you should consider it."

"No...it's not," she said, more soberly. "Why can't you return?"

"I lost my family as well," I said. "But...it was after I had already chosen this life. Look—Fersa, maybe you are better suited to be a wolf. That might always be true. But I think you're capable of learning everything I'm trying to teach you."

"You're just trying to flatter me now. Well, we're both just sitting here every day, pretending to be something we're not. Have you ever seen children put clothes on the cats and dogs? They look ridiculous. That's us, aye? Ridiculous."

She looked at me in a way I was no longer accustomed to, with the penetrating gaze of a wolf, and her nostrils slightly flared as she noticed my scent. Her human nose was not as keen, but wolves could never lose their awareness of such things. She knew I was only pretending to be this man. I might pretend to be a human scholar until the day I died. I would still *always* be a wolf trapped in a tidy and uncomfortable jacket, neatly buttoned vest, and cravat. Trapped by my own choices, my own mistakes.

As she was trapped by misfortune, this lovely girl who was treading on dangerous waters with me, forcing me to come close to reckoning with what I had become, and the devastation I left in my wake.

Why had my brothers kidnapped a princess? Or was it all a misunderstanding? Why did King Brennus kill them? If I touch this girl, I might be accused of the same things...

She was wearing a gown of green today, with red ribbons criss-crossing her bodice, like a branch of holly plucked for the indoors. Too beautiful to be ridiculous.

I could not forget that, on paper, I was a nobody hired to tutor the daughter of one of the wealthiest men in town. I could not forget the human world I had become a part of.

Her eyes briefly flashed a brighter gold. A challenge. Her cheeks were flushed pink. I didn't need to be in the mating season to know exactly what she wanted. A good tussle of fur and teeth and then—

"Miss Fersa," I said. "I think you are forgetting yourself."

She dug her fingernails into the cushion. "Do you not feel it, then? You don't have the high voice of a man who's lost his balls."

I slammed my hands on the table. "Do you want me to have my way with you? And can you explain it to your father if I did?"

"I—I can hardly help feeling what I feel. Wolves don't—that is— Wolves act on their feelings right away."

"Then, you had probably best get married as soon as you can. It's all acceptable once the ring's on your finger. But it won't be to me." I huffed. "Your stepmother may have told you, I'm going to give you an extra lesson this evening. The one I promised you." I stacked up my books and gathered up the papers where she had been scratching out letters and leaving ink blots everywhere. "Maybe we should adjourn for now. I'll return when the sun goes down. I expect you to behave yourself better than you've done today. I suggest a cold bath and some chamomile tea to calm yourself down."

Chapter Six

F ERSA

I WAS RESTLESS AFTER THAT, in a way that made no sense. My body *must* be responding to him simply because he was the only wolf I'd been around since I grew into a woman. My instincts ought to respond to a man who would make a good mate for me, but that couldn't possibly be a strange wolf like him.

I couldn't quite hold back some urge to please him. I was supposed to change clothes for dinner in the evening, as if getting dressed once wasn't enough.

"Is there a special way to get dressed if you want to look nice?" I asked Ina.

"Like what, miss?"

"I don't know. I feel like I've heard of girls taking extra care when they get dressed, but what do they do?"

"They tie their stays tighter."

"*What*? I'll *die* if they're tied any tighter than this."

Ina laughed. "Miss, I suppose I could put your hair up. Someone ye hopes to impress?"

"Yes, I want Mr. Arrowen to think I'm good at being human. Maybe he'll stop harassing me about learning things." I gave my reflection an exasperated look.

"Just make sure Mrs. Rafferty knows you're not a-courtin'." Ina put up my hair with some combs and tied it with a red ribbon. I was a little afraid to move my head now. The dress was a chocolate brown velvet, almost as soft and warm as fur, with white ruffles at the wrists and around my breasts. Ladies didn't have to cover their breasts in the evening. It was all very confusing. I threw my red cloak on over everything and slipped out my gloved hands.

Mr. Arrowen met me in the room where family met guests. I think it was a parlor—or was it the drawing room? I got them all mixed up sometimes.

He had a book in his hand, and was dressed for the cold weather in a coat and hat and gloves. "It won't be long," he told Katherine. "I know Miss Fersa must be back for dinner."

He held open the door and nodded to me. I slipped out past him, my stiff petticoats knocking into his trousers. I tried to hold them closer, but my underthings forced the skirts wide, like it or not. I shoved them back down with a grimace. "Damn things."

He shut the door behind us. "You don't even try, do you?"

"Oh, I'll try when I go to this yule ball business. You'd be surprised if you saw me going out with Mrs. Rafferty. I hardly say a word. And I'm supposed to go to church tomorrow. Have you ever been to church?"

"Wolvenfolk aren't really church-going, are they?"

"Well, that doesn't mean much where you're concerned."

"I've never gone that far," he said. "It would feel false. But I'm sure Mrs. Rafferty will guide you through anything you need to do. The people of this town seem genuinely committed to their belief in not judging others."

"Yeah...well. It'll feel false to me, too." Now my thoughts were veering back to my mother again. Whenever I thought about my father praying or being thankful to the heavens I just got plain angry, thinking about her death. "So tell me this story I've been waiting for all week."

He walked through the garden, a half-step ahead, but he kept checking that I was all right walking on the crust of ice that coated the snow. It had started to melt and then frozen again. I had new boots—I had new *everything*—and my feet crunched through just fine. He had some kind of contraption set up on a stand, a long wooden case with a glass lens pointing up to the skies.

"When I was young," he said, "I used to look at the stars and the moon."

"Well, who doesn't?"

"Yes. Indeed." He sounded miffed. "But I wasn't like the other wolves. I couldn't stop wondering what was up there."

"What is up there?"

"I could tell you the latest theories, but it's better just to see. Come and get a look." He peered in the smaller end of the contraption and adjusted it a little. "This is a telescope. You'll get to see the moon up close."

I hardly knew what he was talking about, but I decided to humor him.

"Don't touch it. Just lean down."

"I wasn't." I crouched a little until I could see through the telescope.

I was startled by the clear vision of a pale sphere marked with what looked like...a landscape. The face of the waxing moon, nearly full, was clear and alien. "It's...it's...it looks lonely." I shivered.

"Aye...not always entirely pleasant to look at the sky. Makes one feel small."

I noted that his speech was slipping into the cadence of the woods, more like mine. He couldn't help it out here in the fresh air, I thought.

I kept gazing at the moon, and the longer I looked, the more I wanted to keep looking. "But that's why you became a scholar?"

"To make a long story short, yes, the sky is what got me asking questions, and my kin didn't know the answers. One day, we went into town to trade with the humans, and there was a man there with a telescope. He asked me if I wanted to see the moon, just like you've seen it today. Of course I said yes, and...well, it was so surprising. So beautiful. I asked him a hundred questions before my mother pulled me away. From then on, when we traded with the humans and I asked them, they would tell me things here and there. Or they'd say, 'You could ask so-and-so, he has some education.' Every little piece of learning I picked up was like a treasure to me. I didn't have any way of writing them down, but I held them all in my head when I was a boy."

"So you *were* part of a wolf clan."

A flash of something dark stirred in his eyes. "Yes. But I left when I was fifteen and got an education from a human man of considerable learning."

"I thought you might have been raised by a human relative."

He shook his head. "I have no human relatives."

"No?" I cried, surprised. I gave his arm a light smack with the back of my glove. "You're more wolf than I am! I hardly believe it!"

"No one does..."

"I'm sorry. I s'pose they didn't always treat you kindly in your clan, then?"

The small, disdainful grunt he made as he peered into the telescope again answered the question. "Do you want to look again?" he asked me. "It's pointing at another planet now."

"Another planet?" I peered at the small red orb. With the naked eye, it looked like a star, but now I could see it like a clouded glass marble.

"It's another world, like ours, so the scholars think."

"Really? Do people live there?"

"No one knows," he said, his hand close to mine, keeping the telescope steady. "And quite likely, we'll never know the answers."

"Oh? Then what's the point of all that?"

"The mystery is eternally intriguing. Maybe we will come to understand some sliver of it that we didn't understand before. That's why I keep looking."

"You really are a *very* strange wolf."

"In some ways. In other ways...I'm more of an ordinary wolf than I let on."

I met his eyes and edged my hand closer to his until our gloved fingers touched. He was still. "Miss Fersa..." His voice turned husky.

"How come you're Mr. Arrowen and I'm Miss Fersa? I don't know your real name." Wolves had family names and clan names, but they were always words describing family attributes and the forest landscape where they lived. I had been Fersa of the Bright Spirit family, of the Blue Pines clan. So I guessed 'Arrowen' was made up.

"Agnar."

A pleasantly familiar wolf name. My clan had an Agnar before I was born. Agnar the River Hunter, they called him, because he would stand in the river and catch fish in his jaws. "Can I call you Agnar, then?"

"It's not how things are done. But during our lessons...why not." He slowly drew his hand back from mine.

I grinned at the withdrawing hand. "Took you a while, though."

"You're asking for trouble for both of us," he said. "Let me take you inside."

"I don't think I need to be taken somewhere that's already within spitting distance. Go home, then, Agnar, if you think I'm so much trouble."

"You *are*." He gave me a brief look, eyelids lowering, and I started walking to the door. I heard him give up on me, boots turning toward the front gate.

I scooped up a handful of icy snow and pitched it at the back of his head.

He growled, whirling on me. I laughed and dove behind one of the bushes as he reached for retaliation. I scooped up another handful, the cold seeping through my gloves and numbing my fingers. He edged around the bushes to get me in his sights.

A snowball exploded on my hair. I felt the ribbon go askew.

I tossed one back at him, right in the face. Aye, you do learn to play dirty in the work house.

His hands, larger than mine, hastily scooped up a big clump of snow and threw it at me. It started breaking apart midair but the remains of it slogged me right in the cleavage. My cloak was flung back at this point, and ice trickled down inside my stays.

"Now you are a cad!" I cried, rushing him, knocking him to the ground.

He easily flipped me onto my back and pinned me down in the snow. I could feel my body prickling with an urge to change and wrestle him, to feel the nip of his teeth in my fur before we succumbed to desire. I struggled for deep breaths in the confines of my clothing, puffs of frost clouding the air between us.

He was breathing hard too, his fingers around my wrists, his warm body pressing into mine, his hard shaft pressing against my pelvis through his trousers. For a moment, we were silent and his lust for me was so raw I thought he might lose control. I knew if he did, he would probably be sent away, and I would be in trouble.

But wolves have a hard time thinking beyond the moment. No matter what my logical human mind told me, my animal brain was on the brink of overruling her.

He shoved me away, violently, and stood up. The silhouette of his disheveled hair glowed under the moonlight. "You will ruin everything for me," he hissed.

"Wait—oh, come on now, we're only having a little fun— you bastard." I quickly sat up and pulled my cloak around my body. "Don't be like that."

"I have fought tooth and nail for every scrap of this life I've built," he said. "To be treated as *human*."

"As a boring old human bachelor who teaches girls their letters? La di da. If that's what you want, then."

"*Obviously* it's what I want."

The front door flung open and the boys came dashing out the door.

"They saw you throwing snowballs out the windows," Father said. "I'll assume the lesson's done. I said they could come play for a bit. It is a beautiful night." He stood on the stoop, lighting a cigar.

Agnar shoved his hands through his hair, taming his fierce expression. He formed a fresh snowball, turning his attention away from me. "Is this a fair fight? I don't know if these little pups can hit me."

"*I* can," Francis said, with scrappy confidence. His gloves clamped around the snow, going straight for the largest snowball his hands could form.

"*Me too!*" John screamed. The other two eagerly followed

his lead. Soon they were ganging up on my tutor, pelting him with snow, while Agnar pretended to fall to their assault.

My eyes blurred, imagining what kind of father he'd make as I watched him pelt the boys with gentle snowballs and make them laugh. Old bachelor! What wolf had ever declared themselves an old bachelor? Why did he have to push me away?

I turned to the door.

"Tired already?" Father asked.

"No, not tired, but I suppose I had better keep my clothes clean," I said, with vague sarcasm.

My stupid body still wanted Agnar so badly that it was like a physical ache. Aye, just my body, I told myself. Certainly not my heart—or god forbid, my *head*. I didn't really care if he didn't come back on Monday after our argument. I wasn't going to toss and turn all night thinking about him. I wasn't going to have the letters he'd taught me dancing in my head, nor the sight of the moon and worlds beyond.

Chapter Seven

FERSA

I DID NOT WAKE up a wolf that morning, because I never slept deep enough to dream of running through the forests on four legs.

Damnit.

I got up when the servants were only just getting the fires going and got dressed on my own.

Sure, they told me not to go out into town alone, but my patience for rules had run out. I needed to be by myself, and I needed to be outside. I crept down the stairs, picked my cloak off the stand in the hall, and slipped out the heavy doors.

It was such a relief, just to be free! I was not exactly alone, because other people were walking down the streets as well, but they were mostly servants at this hour and minding their own business. No one was telling me not to slouch, or correcting my speech. The sun was just creeping up over the sea in the east.

I reached the end of our street and looked both ways. A few carriages trotted by. Most people were on foot, walking up from the docks and markets. The town was built on an incline, so if I turned left, I went uphill toward the forest, but it was still far away. If I turned right, I could see the ships and the ocean.

People nodded at me in a friendly way as I walked by. "Good afternoon and God bless ye, Red Hood!" One of the distant Rafferty aunties greeted me. "What are you doing out alone before church?" I just shrugged.

Street vendors were singing out their various calls: "Oysters and clams, fresh today!" "Rosemary and thyme, get it early before it's gone!" Servants were buying fresh food for Sunday dinners. A brisk wind blew off the sea, tugging at my red cloak, and I pulled it close around me.

I walked all the way down to the docks, where I no longer saw anyone I knew. A line of gray clouds was slowly moving in with the wind, and fishing boats were sailing out. Ropes creaked and waves slapped the sides of the ships. Beyond the ships and men was the ocean, endless and churning. I knew I should probably turn back, but I was somewhat fascinated to stand at the edge of civilization. It reminded me of looking at the moon. I walked all the way to the end of an empty dock, lined with a few shacks, and spread my arms, feeling the wind in my clothes and hair.

"What're ye doing out here, lass?" An old human man in an oiled, fisherman's coat called out to me. "Little Red Hood," he continued. "I've heard of ye. Ye looking for something, starin' out at the sea?"

"I guess we all are." I started to walk back up the dock, past him.

He followed me. "Yer the wolfkin girl, aren't ye?"

"Fersa Rafferty," I said. It was the first time I had invoked my father's name as my own. I was getting nervous, but I told myself that this was a safe place. These were good people here. He wouldn't hurt me.

A hand grabbed my cloak and dragged me back. He pushed me against one of the weathered clapboard shacks. "I heard ye wolfkin girls like to fuck. When the moon's full ye can hardly help it."

I shook my head frantically. My skin was getting very hot, my ribs jabbed by my stays with every quick breath. "No," I said. "That's a myth. It's just once a year in the winter."

"So when's that? It's almost winter..." He pinned my wrists against the wall and rubbed his erection against me. "Might as well get a jump on it, eh?"

"Back the fuck off," I said. As a girl, I was so weak compared to a man. And all my stupid *clothes*. My panic spiked, my instincts screaming. *Don't—don't—*

"Ah, no need for that kind of talk, Miss Rafferty. Have pity on a poor man, would ye? I'll be good to ye." He shoved my wrists together and gripped them both in one brawny hand so he could unleash his cock from his trousers.

My instincts realized that this was only going to go one of two ways. I didn't even hesitate. I slipped into my wolf form. I'd be damned if he was going to take advantage of me.

He was so startled that he immediately let go of my hands, but I had my own problems. I was still wearing my fine clothes. The stays were much too small for the thicker chest of a wolf. The laces of the stays strained open but didn't break, as the shoulders of my dress split reluctantly. My petticoats hampered my legs and the hood of my cloak fell forward, blocking my sight. I tried to run but I didn't want to plunge off the dock. It was hard to breathe.

I heard the shed door swing open and some jostling. He might be looking for a weapon. He grabbed my cloak and it tore away from me. At least I could see now. I twisted back to bite him and managed to tear his shirt but I held back from actually ripping his arm off. This was my only home, my only family. Would the people of Pennarick be so kind if I killed a man? Even in self defense?

He jabbed my side with something sharp that pierced my skin. "Back off, wolf!"

I howled with pain and tried to run for it again, struggling with the skirts. I heard his footsteps behind me and the weapon jabbed me again.

"Hey!" I heard Patrick shout in the distance. He came running, swinging one of the poles the fishermen used to hook and pull their catch. "What's going on?"

When I saw him, I turned back into a girl and clutched my bleeding side. "This bastard tried to fucking rape me!" I didn't feel like softening my language one bit right now.

The fisherman cowered when he saw Patrick coming, lifting his hands. "No, sir, I swear, I wasn't going to hurt her. 'Twas all a misunderstanding."

"She's *bleeding*." Patrick swung the pole at him and knocked him off the dock. He splashed into the cold water and screamed, swimming for a rope ladder that hung down some distance away.

"Well, he knows how to swim, so I'm sure he'll manage," Patrick said, holding a hand down to me. I took it, holding my tattered dress together with my other hand.

"I shouldn't have come here. I didn't know there were any men like that in town." I was more furious than scared.

"You do get rough ones by the docks," Patrick said. "Workers for hire who travel around. The rest of it's safe enough. C'mere, lass, let's get you home. You're lucky I was here. Hold this, and I'll hold you." He handed me the axe, although it was quite heavy. When I took it, he scooped me into his arms. I had never felt so...small. And feminine. It was a strange feeling.

"You're out before the church bells are ringing. Just needed some time to yourself, eh?" he asked.

"Mmhm..." I didn't know what to say.

"You need someone to take care of you," he said.

"I've always taken care of myself just fine."

"But you were a wolf, then. Now, you're a girl. And if you want to stay a girl, you should have a good husband who will walk with you and protect you." He winked. "But I'll let you consider that a while. Let's get you home for now."

I was still disturbed at the idea that I was so fragile I must have a husband accompanying me everywhere. "Yes..."

"I'll explain everything to your father when we get to the house."

That was exactly how it went. Patrick smoothed everything over for me. It was clear that he had a level of authority I did not possess. If he said I needed to be outside for my health, everyone believed him.

Besides that, there was a lot of little secretive smiling between Father and Katherine and Patrick.

"I'll see you at church," Patrick said, tipping his hat before he left.

"Who knows?" Katherine said. "Maybe jingle bells in December will lead to wedding bells in April. Poor dear. Let's get you bandaged up quickly! It doesn't look too deep..."

I needn't have worried about going to church. It wasn't as religious as I expected. I mean, there was a sermon, but it was more like storytelling and talking about concepts like kindness and being neighborly. It didn't make me think about Mother's death too much, as I had feared. More than anything, it was social. The young ladies were all dressed up, and the young men as well, with invitations for carriage rides home flying around. And of course, Patrick kept looking at me all morning.

"Mr. and Mrs. Rafferty. Miss Fersa. I hope you're feeling

better." He approached us, giving me a small bow, after the sermon. "Might I have the pleasure of escorting you home?"

My father and Katherine looked so pleased, and Patrick was looking so handsome in his Sunday best that I nodded. The snowball fight with Agnar seemed like a long time ago after the scare this morning. And after all, everyone wanted me to be with Patrick, it seemed. It was easier for me to see myself with someone from the wolvenfolk, but I was half human, too, and oddly enough, Patrick actually seemed more physical than Agnar. My body thrilled when he put his big hands around my waist and swung me up into his carriage. Not like it did around Agnar, but...maybe that was the way of human courtships. Maybe they always took more time. He tucked the blanket around me.

"Warm enough?"

"Plenty warm."

"Yes, you're a tough little lass, aren't you?"

He understood. Maybe Patrick Rafferty was the man for me, after all. And the town looked so pretty from here behind Patrick's fast horses. Houses and trees were covered in snow. The windows of the shops were decorated with holly and juniper, pine and fir. Chickadees were perched in the bare branches of the bushes in neighborhood gardens. Patrick drove us the long way along the High Road, with a view of the whole harbor.

"Do you want something to fight?" Patrick asked after a moment.

The question surprised me. "What do you mean?"

"I want to go look for the white wolf. Some people have seen him around here."

"Oh—really?"

"So they say. I haven't seen him for myself, but I'll find him. You could track him, couldn't you?"

"Are you actually asking me to turn into a wolf? And track my own kind?"

"'Your own kind'? Well, he's a traitor. He killed the sacred stag and kidnapped the queen."

"I thought that was his brothers who kidnapped the queen?"

"They're a bad lot, either way. His own clan wants him dead, they say. You don't need to defend him."

"I wasn't defending him. I'm just not sure if—"

"It's a hefty reward," he said. "You could really start a life with a purse like that..." His long leg pressed against mine.

I flushed.

"Something inside you wants out, doesn't it?" he said. "Think about it. We have to take him alive."

"He might hurt me..."

"I'm a good shot with a bow. I'd cover you and stick him in a spot that isn't fatal."

"No arrows," I said quickly. "Please."

He paused and I think he knew I meant; maybe he had heard the story of my mother. "All right, lass, no arrows. Of course I don't want to kill him. I can bring a net and a tranquilizer. But that's just details. The point of it is to feel the wind and the rush..."

I did want to feel that. *The hunt.* Yes, I missed that. I'd just never hunted another wolf before.

As if he anticipated my apprehension, Patrick said, "Fersa, someone's going to get that wolf. It might as well be us. We won't hurt him, and we won't use the reward for anything nefarious. Just imagine the kind of people who are probably salivating over that fifty gold."

"Would Father and Katherine let me do something like that?"

"No, I don't think they would," he said, laughing. "I've

thought of that. You'll go pay a visit to your grandmother, and while you're there, we'll meet up for the hunt."

"My grandmother?"

"You haven't heard the tale of your grandmother? Ask your father about her. I think you'll be happy to pay her a visit once you hear it."

"Your grandmother...," Father murmured.

I brought it up as soon as Patrick brought me home. Father stuffed his hands in his pockets. "Shouldn't be Patrick's business, but he does seem to have a liking to the old girl. I suppose I should tell you about her sooner rather than later..."

"Oh, come on! I'm only getting more curious!"

"I told you my grandfather was a hard man. I told you I ran away. I didn't tell you about the other link in the chain. I don't want to encourage you! But—when my father died, and I ran away, my mother ran after me. Well, she ran into the woods, at any rate. You can only imagine—it was a disaster for my grandfather's reputation. Grandson and daughter both running off into the forest? Eventually I came back, as I said. It wasn't easy. I truly loved your mother. I really had to behave myself when I got back, mind you. We're quite forgiving here, but every tongue in town was wagging about what I'd done."

"But...your mother?" I pressed.

"Yes. Mother...when I got back, she had moved into an old cabin in the woods, and she refused to come back. She lives there to this day. She's getting older now, but she won't budge. Still chopping wood..." He shook his head, his eyes fond. "I admire her, but she worries me to death. She's so alone out there, Fersa. I don't want you to be alone."

"Can I meet her?"

"We'll go see her when the winter snows end," he said.

My eyes drifted to the window. Snow was drifted against the pane. "She really lives all alone out there in the snow? And she's a human?"

"We're not *that* helpless." He patted my head in an absent, tender gesture like I was one of the boys. "That's no place for anyone who isn't half crazy, which I fear your grandmother might just be, even if she hides it well enough."

"You'd let her be all alone during the yuletide season?" I'm not sure I was very good at imploring eyes, but I tried my best. Now I wanted to meet this grandmother of mine, no matter my plans with Patrick.

"She's bound and determined to be out there," he said.

"But I can't go see her? Father—you know how much I miss the woods. Maybe it would help if I could spend just a little time out there, talking to another woman who has been torn between the town and the wilds. But I could help her, too. I'm young and strong. If she needed help with anything at the cabin to prepare for winter, I could do it. And there's a rogue wolf out there. You just said you worry about her."

"I do," he admitted.

"Please?"

He paused. "After the yuletide ball, you can go visit her. Patrick Rafferty has already asked me if he could take you."

"Oh, did he? He didn't ask me."

"He will. It's proper for him to ask *my* permission first."

I rolled my eyes. "All right."

Chapter Eight

FERSA

I WAS TREMENDOUSLY EXCITED to have an escape plan. When Agnar showed up on Monday, I dreaded my lessons more than ever.

"I didn't even know if you'd come back," I told him, when the door shut behind him. "You seemed so cross at me yesterday."

"It's a good position," he said, idly brushing his fingers on the keys of the piano in the corner.

"Do you play?" I asked.

"No. I don't really understand music."

"Really? It's so beautiful."

"That is one area where I'm all animal, I suppose, much to my regret."

"Well, there had to be something," I said, adding, "Don't worry about what I said the other day. My cousin will be asking me to the yuletide ball, so there you are. I won't push myself on you again."

"Patrick Rafferty?" he asked, his voice getting a whispery edge, like a blade being sharpened.

"Aye...you know him?"

"He's a hunter."

"Yes, I guess he is. Are you going to the ball?"

"I was invited. I may go just to say hello since they were kind enough to extend the invitation. I don't get that many of them."

I suddenly felt awkward. "We're halfway through the alphabet, aren't we?" I picked up his case of books myself, trying to change the subject.

"He wants to find that white wolf..."

"I would never want to hurt another wolf," I said. "Except that wolf is wanted by his own clan *and* King Brennus. They said the very spirit of the forest asked King Brennus to hunt him down."

"I know, but I still have a hard time condemning another wolf, knowing how many of our kind have been killed and persecuted by elves and humans."

"How can we argue with the very forest itself?"

"That's true," Agnar admitted. "The blue stag is very beautiful and very rare."

"Indeed," I said, relieved that he wasn't judging me for it. But then we both lingered a moment in silence.

"The fertile moon will be coming soon," he said, when the pause grew very long.

"The fertile moon! I haven't heard it called that before. Well, you don't have to worry about the fertile moon. I'm going away to visit my grandmother in the woods during the heat."

"Ah. Well, be careful of stray wolves in the woods."

"Naturally. I'm not some bitch with no control at all. I'm not taking up with some rogue." No, I'd have Patrick to keep my mind off that.

Yes. Yes, I'd have Patrick.

Agnar, I thought, could at least bother being a little jealous.

It hit me suddenly that it was all I wanted. For Agnar to demand that I accept his invitation to the ball instead. After all, Patrick hadn't actually asked *me* yet, just Father.

Agnar handed me a piece of paper, and the quill, and formed some letters as an example, talking for a bit about what sound they matched. He told me to write them out. I did, trying to copy his controlled loops. My hands seemed a little unusually clumsy. Maybe because he was sitting behind me and staring at them as I wrote.

I stopped, shoving an errant lock of hair out of my eye. "Well, don't breathe down my neck, I'm *trying*."

Warm hands suddenly clutched my shoulders, his forehead pressing into the back of my skull. Now he really was breathing down the back of my neck. "Fersa...you're not going to a dance with that blood-hungry bastard."

"If you know something about him that I don't, you'd better tell me now," I said, even as I relished his touch, heat rushing from his hands all down my spine and between my legs. If I was in full heat, I wondered if I'd have any control at all. "Has he hurt other wolvenfolk?"

His fingers tightened on my skin.

"Well? Has he?"

"No, it's—it's my intuition," he said.

"I think it might actually be something else," I said.

"What's that?"

I looked back at him over my shoulder. "Jealousy."

"Jealousy? You think I am swayed by mere jealousy?"

"I'm disappointed if you're not, actually."

He growled a little, and then he pulled my mouth against his. He was a little rough and it was exactly what I wanted. I wanted rough, I wanted passionate, I wanted a lack of tedious human rules and controlled emotions. I wanted to fuck like forest beasts.

His tongue shoved into mine, and I shoved back, his hands still gripping me from behind, but now he pulled me off the stool and onto his lap, his hard cock against my ass—well, through an annoying sea of skirts. I clutched my bodice, wishing it was easier to rip it all off, but after a moment I succumbed to the fact that I couldn't, and reached back to grab a fistful of his hair, holding him against me. Our tongues wrestled the way I wished our entire bodies would.

He drew back after such a long kiss that my lips felt a little swollen. I was sure he was going to say something to ruin it, a "We shouldn't" or "They'll hear us"—although no one was home but the servants right now—or "Woman, have you no shame?"

"Is this what you want?" he asked, nudging his cock against me.

"Yes..."

He tore aside the sheer cloth that covered my cleavage, and he slipped his fingers under the edge of my clothes. He lifted my breasts up so the nipples were exposed over my low-cut dress, and twisted them in his fingers, dropping kisses down my bare neck. I shivered. "Oh, sweet trees and flowers, yes...," I breathed. I spread my legs as his rough touch built up my desire. Maybe these clothes had a certain allure. Seeing his large ink stained hands invading the ruffles and lifting up my breasts like treasures he was surfacing from the bed of the ocean, I was more aroused than ever. I imagined how long it would take him to strip off all the pieces and discover all my naked skin. I imagined his hands traveling over all of the smooth surfaces of my human self, and then we would shift and discover each other all over again.

He played with my breasts until I was begging for more

LIDIYA FOXGLOVE

and then he pulled up my skirts roughly with a growl of pure lust, finding my naked pussy underneath.

"No underthings?" he grunted.

"Only ten thousand petticoats. No one gave me anything else."

"Do any of these girls wear underwear in this town?"

"Probably not the custom, is it?"

"Is that so?" He groaned, stroking me a moment, and then I felt him unbuttoning his trousers under me, letting his rigid manhood spring out to meet me. *Now, you're thinking like a wolf,* I thought, almost giddy that I had broken him. *Yes, my sweet scholar, I know what you really are.*

"I want you," he said. "You should be mine."

"I am yours."

"Not Patrick's." He looked at me with his eyelids heavy, blinking with lust, his golden eyes like low flames. His hair was mussed, and I couldn't resist stroking one of his sideburns with the side of my hand. "Fersa, promise me you won't go with him."

I paused. "Father expects it..."

He slid his cock between the lips of my pussy, teasing me with penetration. He grabbed my knees and spread them wider. "I don't trust Patrick Rafferty. Promise me."

I was going half insane with wanting him, but at the same time, Father expected so much of me. "He saved me the other day."

"Aye, and he wants something from you." He lifted me up by the waist and shoved my skirts down. He gave me a measured look. "I won't risk my reputation for you unless you promise me..."

"Oh?" Before he could button his trousers, I took his cock in my hand and stroked the entire length, once and then twice, tightening my grip on the second. A bead of liquid appeared at the tip.

His whole body twitched like he was about to grab me and shove me against the table. I knelt and wrapped my mouth around his cock. My breasts were still lifted over the edge of my dress, and I made sure he could see them too, lifting them up to him as I slicked my tongue over the head.

He gripped the table. "You little bitch."

"So I am," I said, before I took his length down into my throat, sliding my tongue all along his skin. I was spurred on by the pained growl he made. I pulled my mouth back and hugged his cock between my breasts. "You're a wolf, Agnar. It's a crime for you to be anything else."

"Curses..."

I resumed my work, up and down his shaft until I knew he was helpless to resist. I knew he was incapable of stopping me now and the thought that I had done this to me only encouraged me. He grabbed a fistful of my hair and took control, stroking his cock along my tongue and clenching a handful of one of my bare breasts. He wasn't gentle anymore. Wolves weren't gentle. I tasted him, all sweet musk and male flesh. I was starving for him.

Somewhere in the house, a door shut and I heard Katherine call for some servant. I stiffened with panic and he held my head, his seed spurting into my mouth as he let out a low moan, digging his fingers deeper into my hair, stroking my scalp. I licked my lips, savoring every drop, missing the wild, earthy tastes of an animal life. Then he withdrew quickly, buttoning his trousers, as I swallowed hard, one palm on the floor.

"I want more," I whispered.

He looked down at me with a wild look. "I would never have done that if you hadn't—" He sputtered, "I could lose —*everything*. Everything, again."

I stood up, punching my skirts into place. "Again?"

"I already lost my clan because I wanted to learn. They've shunned me. This is all I have now."

"Well, I don't shun you for learning," I said. "I just—can't ignore this feeling."

He reached for my hand. "I have resisted this for a long time. But—it does grow more difficult every day. Maybe it's time to settle down. If I could have your hand properly..."

"You could ask me to the dance, Agnar. Before Patrick does."

"It would raise eyebrows."

"Well, what are you thinking you'll do then? You're very confusing. And to be honest, sometimes I think Patrick understands me better than you do."

"Impossible," he snapped.

"When I go to visit my grandmother, will you meet me in the woods? Will you run with me, as a wolf?"

He winced. "If I did—"

"If you're really a wolf, and you really accept that side of me, you'd better think of some way to prove it."

Chapter Nine

FERSA

BY THE NIGHT of the yule ball, I was full of anxiety and excitement. Agnar kept coming for lessons but he was so distant now that I couldn't find any way to crack him, unless perhaps if I shoved my hand down his trousers (which I was very tempted to do). I was so annoyed with him that I thought Patrick's company would be a relief.

I was starting to come into heat, that was certain. It stirred inside me gently at first, a rising sense of wild abandon. My sense of smell grew stronger, even in human form. All the men tonight were going to smell delicious, I thought. Patrick included.

I was a little worried I would have a hard time maintaining control, but when I looked in the mirror I just looked small and almost sweet in my gown, with a necklace of blue stones Katherine let me borrow. Katherine and Father were both dressed in their best, and so was I. We took the carriage down streets that glowed with lantern-light cast on sparkling snow. It was so enchanting that I felt like a princess myself. *I do need to learn to write so I can tell Ellara about this,* I thought.

But thoughts of writing just gave me that annoying urge to show Agnar I was as good as him. I didn't want to be a scholar with superior airs who forgot what being a wolf was like, and yet I couldn't seem to help competing with him, hating him a little bit for knowing so much more than I did—and wanting him, more than anything or anyone.

"You look like something's troubling you," Katherine said. "On such a night? It's going to be great fun."

"No, nothing's troubling me."

"You seem to get along very well with Patrick," Father said, with a hint of hopefulness.

"I do. It's not Patrick. I'm fine." I really wasn't used to having people paying so much attention to my moods and asking me so many questions about my future.

The dance was held in a great hall that usually functioned as sort of a gentleman's club, but tonight it was for everyone. The white brick building was splendidly decorated with wreaths and greenery. Lanterns blazed all along the approach. The carriage dropped us off at the entrance. The air smelled of woodsmoke. Everyone was merry and comparing dresses. A servant took my cloak.

I wished I had some female friends here. The younger girls in town had mostly avoided me. I tugged at the fingers of my gloves, watching them all chattering while I stood by the wall.

Patrick rescued me with a gallant bow. "You look beautiful tonight."

"So do you. Handsome, I mean." I couldn't help grinning. He was wearing a green coat with gold buttons, but he had not groomed his hair or thrown on cologne as much as some of the other men. He looked ready to escape.

"Crowded in here," he said.

"Yes..."

"I don't love large gatherings much. Nor these dances. I hear your lessons are going well, though?"

"Aye, I do like dancing."

"Then I will make sure you have plenty of dancing tonight. But I'm looking forward to our escape." He winked.

He wants something from you. Agnar's voice was in my head. Curse him. My intuition was surely as good as his, and I didn't feel any sense of wrongness with Patrick.

The only trouble, really, was the rising strength of my desire. A part of me liked the courting and the teasing. I just wondered how long I could stand it.

We each had a cup of syllabub, sweet and frothy and heady, and Patrick introduced me to some friends of his with his hand around my shoulders. Then he led me to the dance floor, our arms extended in one graceful line, as other couples did the same. I had to concentrate hard on the steps I'd practiced, walking around him and curtseying before he took me in his arms. He gazed at me like he was enchanted.

Over his shoulder, I saw Agnar having a glass of wine, standing next to an old suit of armor.

I stumbled.

"Sorry—"

"It's all right," Patrick said. "You're quite a good dancer, actually."

"I'm probably not used to drinking."

"A girl who can't hold her liquor should be careful. Some gentlemen might take advantage."

"They'll have to get past you first, won't they?"

"Ha! That's right." He spun me around. "Fersa...you're so...refreshing."

I blushed. "That's just another word for 'strange', isn't it?"

"I can't wait to have you all to myself."

That sobered me a little. He assumed we were as good as

married already, it seemed. "You're not worried that I might turn into a wolf and bite you?"

He laughed harder, and a blonde girl dancing by looking at him curiously. "I think I can handle you. I like my girls dangerous, not kept like hothouse flowers. I'm very much looking forward to our hunt."

I hoped Agnar couldn't hear us from his vantage point. Wolves had good ears. "Shh. I don't want my father and Katherine catching wind of our plans."

"They're all the way over there!" He gestured and yes, they were all the way across the room. He must have sensed wariness in my tone. "Afraid for your reputation? It won't matter when you're mine. We're well matched. Maybe other men are afraid to share their bed with a girl who might turn into a wolf, but I'm not. I'll keep your instincts well tamed, lass."

"Oh my." I tried to sound demure. I didn't really want to be tamed, did I? My yearning little body still responded as if it did, growing hot in all the right places.

Of course, my body just wanted everything right now. And it was only going to get worse in days to come.

Chapter Ten

AGNAR

SHE *KNEW* wolves had sharp hearing.

And she must have known I could not help but pay attention.

Did she know what she was saying?

She was going to hunt a fellow wolf.

After she had lost her own family to the elves? Didn't she stop to consider that maybe the white wolf didn't deserve his fate either?

My pulse was racing, sweat soaking my shirt. I was suddenly sharply aware of what a dangerous game I was playing. I was trying to fit in somewhere I would never fit in. I was getting too close to a wealthy man's daughter. I was far too close to her the other night. This would all be difficult enough.

But I was the most wanted man in the entire country.

My little brothers were already dead.

Worse still, soon I would have no choice but to escape

into the forest. The mating season was almost upon me. I was not safe around Fersa. I had come within an inch of fucking her. If she bore my child we would have a very serious problem. But maybe, now, it wasn't safe for more reasons than one. The very idea of her hunting me at Patrick's side made me want to grab her by the arm this very moment, pull her away from him forever, take her back to my humble dwelling, lift her skirts and give her everything she'd already been asking me for. Mark her as my own, now and forever. To see that boorish hunter with his smug smile and his meaty hand on her waist...

I could tear him apart.

She kept dancing with him. I had to remove myself from the room. I had a drink but I didn't dare have two. I needed to keep control.

I can't let this happen. I can't let her go anywhere with him, much less marry him.

It would be so simple, in the moment, to change her mind. She was clearly attracted to me. If I asked her to dance, if I told her I would run with her as a wolf, she would drop Patrick in an instant, wouldn't she?

When she saw me as I truly was, she would know I had dyed my hair black, that I was a wanted man in my other form, and even if not for that, her father would never let her marry a man like me. Patrick was well liked in town, a distant cousin of Fersa's, with an inheritance—everything a human parent would want.

But I couldn't get her out of my head. She haunted my every waking thought these days. I lost sleep for thinking of her scent, the feel of her hair beneath my fingers. When I dreamed, I was tearing through the forest with her on all fours. I was protecting her from all of life's dangers.

This was the feeling a wolf had for his mate. The feeling she had unlocked in me with her tempting and teasing and—

something more. Something I saw in her from the very first moment. My mother used to tell me that someday, I would do anything for my mate, and I would have no control over it. I always got angry when she told me I wouldn't have any control.

But control was an illusion.

I had the sickening sense of my destiny hurtling me toward pain. It was a familiar feeling. I'd first known it when I told my own father I wanted to go to a human school.

I would never forget the way he growled and then laughed. *A wolf? Going to school? They would never accept you!*

It was several years before I was old enough and had enough of my own will that I set out on my own. I left behind my parents and my two small brothers, including little Ergar, who looked up to me like the moon revolved around me. But I had to do it. I set off for the large town of Awn and knocked on the door of a scholar's academy.

The door slammed in my face. Townsfolk glared at me, told me to leave, refused even to sell me a drink. Until I met Alvo Giardi. A traveler and eccentric nobleman, he invited me to travel with him back to his home, a modest estate stuffed with books, specimens of dried flowers and strange insects and shells, and taxidermy. He let me linger on the pages, showed me rare tools for calculating equations and studying the stars, spread maps on tables. He opened the door to a world beyond my dreams—and then he leveled the price.

You're a wolf. A good hunter, eh? I want a blue stag.

My mother said blue stags are special! I could never—

Then, I can't take you in. You have no money. It's all I ask, lad. I've always wanted a blue stag for my collection...

Chapter Eleven

FERSA

AFTER A NUMBER OF DANCES, I was starting to feel a little sick. My desire was twisting into something ravenous and tortured. I'd never gone into heat with men around. Something inside me cried out—not for Patrick, but for Agnar, confusing pain in the ass that he was. "Patrick—actually—maybe I'd better sit down for a minute."

He put a hand on my forehead. "You are warm. Yes, take it easy, lass. There's an empty chair over by your stepmother. I'll be waiting." He kissed my hand.

I walked over, feeling more nauseated by the moment.

"Are you all right?" Katherine asked.

"Mm...just..."

"Too much exercise for a lady's constitution," she declared.

"I've chased rabbits for miles!" I couldn't help but defend myself.

"Well...not in a gown."

"Then...why *do* we wear them?" I clutched my head. It was spinning. Outside the window, the moon was full and bright. Suddenly I felt absolute panic and clutched Katherine's hand. "I need to go."

"Go? We just arrived. Let me get you some—"

"No, please—"

I suddenly felt my entire body break into a cold sweat, and then I started slipping into a contortion. I was changing. I was changing into a wolf in the middle of the yuletide ball with every damn human in town in the room. I garbled out something before my mouth started stretching. My necklace was choking me, my body tearing through another dress. I fell off the chair, my hands scrambling for purchase somewhere. The transformation was not quite complete as I tried to resist it; I must have looked like a monster. I saw Katherine's face looming over me, shrieking.

"Get her out of here!" Father cried.

I tried to get onto my feet, tussling with the dress. I saw Patrick in the crowd. He looked apprehensive. He was not here to save me from a lecherous stranger this time. He couldn't save me from my own self. I saw girls dashing away. I had never felt so small in my entire life. My instincts roared panic. I howled with fear.

No...no!

And then stars filled my vision, and my knees buckled beneath me.

I woke up in my bed, fully human as far as I could see, with Father and Katherine sitting nearby.

"She's awake," Katherine said. "Fersa...sweetheart?"

I trembled at the tender words. She didn't sound angry. I could hardly believe it. "I'm—I'm sorry."

"Ina told us you've been changing into a wolf every morning," Father said. "You should have told us you weren't fully in control."

"I—I thought I was in control as long as I was awake."

"Then what happened?"

Lord, but I didn't want to explain to my father. "Once a year, wolves have a...um...a mating season," I stammered. "I mean, we can mate other times. But at that time it becomes... you know—stronger. I've never been around men since..."

"Oh! That's all it is!" Katherine sounded relieved. "Douglas, why didn't you tell me? You must have known. Mr. Arrowen alluded to it but I didn't really understand it was so serious."

"I'd forgotten."

I covered my face. "I can never—" I stopped, realizing that I was wearing bracelets of silver. I touched my neck and found a silver choker.

Just like I was forced to wear at the work house, to keep me from changing. The jewelry locked around me so I couldn't remove it myself.

"Only until you can control your transformations," Father said. "I'm sorry, Fersa, but...I know you don't want another incident like that one. Isn't it a relief?"

"But I'm supposed to go into the forest to visit my grandmother!"

"Yes, all the more reason! You definitely should not lose control there," he said.

"You had these...sitting around?" I could barely keep from losing it. I wanted to think these people truly loved me. What did they really think, if they had silver cuffs and collar waiting for the moment when my transformation had to be bound? Silver was not cheap enough to buy on a whim. "Take them off! Take them off!"

"Don't be upset, dear, it's a temporary measure,"

Katherine said. "Do they hurt? Is that it? I just don't want you to be embarrassed."

I made a noise of frustration. "They don't hurt. You don't understand!"

Father patted my shoulder. "I think we do, kit. We're just trying to do what's best for you. You can still visit your grand-mother and I think you'll feel a lot better having a respite from all these new experiences. The older you get, the easier it will be to balance all these feelings."

"I'll make you some tea," Katherine said. "Is there anything else that might help?"

"No."

They shut the door and I heard them whispering about me. "She's young..."

"I think we'd better get her married sooner rather than later... I've seen the way she looks at Mr. Arrowen!"

"Patrick could always teach her to read, little by little in the evenings..."

"Can *Patrick* read?" Katherine asked, with a laugh. "He's all muscle, isn't he?"

I slumped onto the pillow, looking at the silver shackles on my wrists, the walls that bound me. *I'll keep your instincts well tamed, lass...*

There was one strange sort of relief to it. Patrick could not ask me to hunt a fellow wolf now.

Chapter Twelve

FERSA

MY FATHER LET me mope in bed a few days, all my tutoring sessions canceled, while he arranged my travel. Grandmother didn't live that far away. Apparently her cottage was along the High Road, once it snaked off into the forest, and you could walk there in a matter of hours. But of course, he said I *must* go in a hired carriage. Ladies didn't walk through the woods unchaperoned. Mercy me.

I had just a small valise packed with what Katherine called "practical" clothing (it had less lace than usual), lunch, and holiday sweets for Grandmother. The coach set off early in the morning, rattling over the roads out of town.

An hour into the journey, we were in the forest. The driver stopped to take a piss. He was already taking out tobacco and I expected he wasn't going to be quick about the break.

While he headed one way, I grabbed my valise and ran the other way.

I ran like I was being chased. I ran until my lungs were bursting against my still very impractical clothing. I ran until I couldn't run any more, savoring the fresh air, the wind on my face, the smell of snow and wild things all around me. The snow was covered in tracks. If only I could turn into a wolf!

But I still had keen senses and I knew how to find my way. I worked my way back to the road, hopping over frigid creeks and falling into unexpected drifts.

Guilt pricked at me. The coachman was going to take the blame for my disappearance and Katherine and Father might be worried. But they ought to be able to guess. I'd protested about the coach already. I needed this time alone in the world that would always be my first home.

I grew reflective as my steps slowed down. Yes, this was my home and so it would always be. I was probably a few days' walk from the forest where I had grown up, from the place my mother died. But it was all part of the same northern sea of green, and it smelled the same; had the same trees and animals. The streams might have been the same ones I drank from before, only closer to where they met the sea. I realized I was shivering, and pulled my cloak tight around me, one frigid hand clutching my valise.

Unfortunately, I couldn't hunt without being able to transform. A simmering anger was building up in me slowly over the fact that my own family would entrap me. I worked up an appetite quickly with all the exercise and cold. The packed lunch was gone quite early and before long I was tempted to eat Grandmother's presents.

I heard something in the distance. A presence, moving softly through the snow.

"Is someone there?" I picked up a large stick. I sniffed the air, trying to pick out a scent on the wind. "Damn it," I cursed, infuriated by my weak human senses.

My eyes skimmed over the forest, and I saw something move. I watched as a wolf approached in the distance.

The white wolf.

Well, *a* white wolf, at least.

He was a male, and he was beautiful, with fur that matched the snow, pristine and soft. His golden eyes were intelligent; I knew he was wolvenfolk and not a pure wolf. He might be dangerous. He might not follow clan laws.

"Sir Wolf...," I breathed. "I'm just passing through."

He stopped at the edge of the path and tilted his head as if to ask me a question.

"I'm visiting my grandmother, that's all."

He took a step closer. His ears were lowered, not quite aggressive, but tense. I was painfully aware that he could have killed me.

"You know I'm a wolf too," I said. "You can smell it. But look—I can't change. It wouldn't be a fair fight, so I hope you'll let me pass."

His eyes seemed a little judgmental.

"You think I wanted this to happen?" I remained still and then held out a hand. "Are you *the* white wolf? The one who made an enemy of the forest itself, and the king of the wood elves? You don't look half as scary as they said."

He sniffed the silver cuff at my wrist.

I snapped it back. I felt weak, to be in this position, to have let this happen at all. "Yes, well."

He looked sympathetic.

"Horrid, isn't it?" I said. "Here I was going to run through the woods with my clothes in my teeth."

He huffed and came closer. I sank my fingers into his soft fur. This was not proper at all, even among wolves. You were not supposed to take a human form and pet a fellow wolf like a dog. But I couldn't resist. I hadn't felt another wolf in a long, long time. I missed the soft, safe feeling of other wolves around me at night. That was so long ago, it seemed like a dream I'd once had.

But this one-sided conversation was getting aggravating.

"You could change back and talk to me," I said. "I've seen plenty of naked men."

He squinted at me.

"You smell familiar...," I said, drawing my hand away.

He made a little warning grunt and took a step back.

"Let me see you," I said.

Now his ears flattened a little.

"Stubborn, are you? Don't look at me like that. I would change if I could and then we'd see what's what." I missed the language of howls and huffs and grunts, ears and tails. It seemed so simple compared to the human world. "I miss being a wolf."

He had rather deep eyes for a wolf, I thought.

I shook my head. "Fine. I don't know what you want. Just let me pass." I started to walk and he leapt onto the path ahead of me, as if to block me. He nudged his head against my skirts.

"Get out of the way."

He stayed in the center of the path, and I nudged him with my stick and went on by. I was a little nervous now, because he was acting so strange and I couldn't change. I was really quite helpless if I started thinking about it. But I wasn't going to show any fear.

Suddenly he tackled me, his massive form hitting me and knocking me onto the soft snow. My valise tumbled out of my hand. I managed to keep hold of the stick, and I tried to whack behind me with it, to beat him back, but no sooner had I started to move than I felt his body shifting on top of mine, and human hands pinned me down.

Chapter Thirteen

Agnar

I watched her from a distance first. My fur blended in with the snow and yet I still took a risk, staying this close to the road. I had to know how she would react if she saw me.

When I saw the silver cuffs on her wrists, I realized there was no other way she could react. They had bound her to her human form before sending her off to the forest. Any wolf could maul her to death if they wished, so of course she was friendly. I knew this must be breaking her heart.

I knew so well.

When I killed the blue stag, Mr. Giardi opened his doors to me. He taught me how to read and write, everything he knew about plants and planets and mathematics and medicine, and how to speak and conduct myself like a human in society.

But he also dyed my hair a dark color and told everyone I was his country nephew. It didn't take long before I realized why. He was a curious man, and I was an object of curiosity.

Could a wolf take to learning? Could a wolf abandon his true nature? That was what he wanted to find out. I was young and I had not known that killing a blue stag was a crime in this land. Once it was done, the true payment I offered him was that I could never leave. I could not be a wolf anymore, not if I wanted to; the locals were keeping an eye out for me.

It's all right, Mr. Giardi said. *You're safe with me.* He was attentive to me, and offered much praise. He spread the stag's pelt on his bedroom floor and mounted its striking black horns above his bed, and after a little while, I started to feel sick whenever I saw them.

One day, I found the notebooks. A dozen of them, little black books, filled with notes on me. All the times I shifted into a wolf or fell into "a temper" or what he called "wild moods", how my eyes seemed to flash gold and I raged and snapped in my struggle to gain control. How much food I ate, and how much I slept, and how tall I was, and how quickly I learned the things he was teaching me. Countless opinions on me: "impetuous", "struggles with abstract concepts", "will probably never be welcomed in royal houses anywhere", "he battles against his animal nature but cannot overcome it".

Up until I found the notes, I thought I was doing a pretty good job of learning, but in the notes I saw myself as I really must be: a failure of a human, but stuck in the guise of one. I gathered my clothes and a few coins he had given me for spending money, hoping he would not accuse me of stealing, and left. I was seventeen at that time. I wandered, asking for work, until I found a country school that needed a teacher, and so my career began. I was far from Mr. Giardi at this point, and I dared to shift my shape a little more often. I ran free in the woods when the workday was over.

That ended this past autumn, when I heard that my little brothers had kidnapped a princess, nearly raped her according to the accounts, and that now King Brennus was looking for me. At first, I didn't believe the reports, but they were corroborated everywhere. *The Longtooth brothers. The Stone Hollow clan. A white wolf...*

And the crime that would haunt me forever, the slaughtered stag.

I didn't know what had become of my brothers in the time after I left them, that they would have become kidnappers. I couldn't believe the story was true, but it seemed that nothing good was likely to come of me either, at this rate.

Mr. Giardi was right, in the end. I had been battling my animal nature since I was a child and I couldn't overcome it now. I knew I would make Fersa mine, even as I knew I might be jailed for it—or worse. I already knew I was bound to her. I could never leave Pennarick. I could hardly stand being apart from her.

The last time I'd seen her, she was dancing with *him*. The very thing I begged her not to do.

I held her wrists in my hands, leaning my weight against her. I was already growing hard with desire for her as she wriggled under me. I dreamed of ripping off her clothes with my hands and teeth and taking her naked right there in the snowbank.

She bit my hand.

"Ugh!" I snapped my hand back.

"Agnar?" She tried to twist back and look at me.

"Who cuffed you?" I asked, pained by the sight of her slim wrists firmly encased in those bands of silver. "Your father? It serves you right. I told you to stay away from Patrick Rafferty."

"I—I didn't know the white wolf was *you*. Your hair is black!"

"Yes. I dyed it so no one would *kill* me."

"But why—why did you kill a blue stag? Or—did you?"

"You're not entirely sure that you believe that poster, then?"

"I can't imagine you would do something so...forbidden. Everyone knows the blue stags are guardians of the forest..."

"So you're not sure? But if you helped Patrick capture me, I would be dragged to the capital in chains and executed, like so many wolves before me. And you would never know the truth."

"I...I... Let me go!"

"Not yet." I kept her pinned under me. "I want to know what is in your head, that you would trust a swaggering young human with an axe over one of your own kind. That you would believe those posters. You know how elves treat wolves. You know, of all people, *you know*! I will not be hunted down, especially by the first woman I've—" I broke off with a growl.

An angry sob ripped out of her throat. "I'm sorry! Then tell me—*why* do they hunt you?"

My grip on her arms finally softened a little, hearing her cry, even if she sounded more furious than anything. "I did kill a blue stag. But I was young. I didn't know just how serious it was. I traded the stag for...an education."

"Who asked you to make a trade like that?"

"He was a lord, a wealthy man of learning from Bondino."

"Were those really your brothers? The other wolves who were killed by King Brennus?"

"Yes," I said. "I don't know what happened or why... They were much younger than me when I left my clan. No older than your little brothers."

"I'm sorry..."

"What matters to me now," I said, right into her ear, "is that you didn't trust me. I need your trust, if we're going to do this. I would never deceive you, Fersa. But I'm a wanted man. If you deceive me, I might be a dead one as well."

She swallowed thickly. "I guess, deep down, I just wanted to belong. And you don't know what you want. One minute you touch me and the next minute you push me away."

My stern demeanor was broken abruptly by a pinecone hitting me right in the back of the head. This sort of thing happened to me all the time when I left town. The forest itself was angry at me for killing one of its guardians.

She almost smiled. "The forest really doesn't like you, eh?"

"No. I am not welcome here anymore," I said, making no effort to hide my bitterness. "I'm lucky the forest can't carry a bow. I only come during this time, when I don't have much choice. I'm afraid I might betray my animal nature..."

Animal nature...yes. Even my human nose could smell the heady aroma of desire—hers and mine.

"You wanted to see me as a wolf. You said this was what I had to prove. Well, here I am. I'm not here to play nice anymore," I said, finally releasing her wrists so my hands could have my fill of other parts of her.

Chapter Fourteen

FERSA

HIS BODY WAS INTIMATELY close to me—and naked. I couldn't see him well with him pinning me, but I felt the warm weight of him. "Then what are we here to play?" I asked.

He made an urgent growl in my ear, spurred on by my words. "I want you to make me that promise. Stay away from Patrick."

"Patrick has never tried to make a lady out of me like you did. He's never criticized my accent or cared that I can't read."

"Because he never cared at all."

"How do you know?"

"He never cared like I did. I know it." He nipped my ear, his breath hot against the winter air. "You remind me of who I used to be...and you make me want to be more than I am now."

"Agnar, please..."

LIDIYA FOXGLOVE

"Aye, how do you want me to please you?" His voice was low, his accent sliding back into the wolfkin tones that were somewhere between human and wood elf with a little something else, something gruff and careless on top of it.

I thought I should probably put up at least some pretense of protest. But I didn't want to. It was stupid to protest. "But aren't you cold? Take my cloak."

"I'm not cold at all. Are you cold at all?"

"No, actually. Not a bit."

He turned my head sideways enough that our lips could meet. He was still pinning me down, his weight not painful but just gently pressing me into the soft snow. His warm mouth was rough against mine, his tongue tasting a little like blood. He'd probably killed his lunch not long before he came across me. The thought of him hunting made me want him all the more. He took my lower lip between his teeth and gently bit me there too, these gentle aggressions assuring me that he was fit to be my mate, a hunter and provider and not just a human toting books around.

"From the moment I walked into the room, I knew," he said. "And you knew. Someday, I was going to fuck you."

"Yes..." My breath hitched.

"And that day is today."

His arms wrapped around me, serpentine, one around my breasts and the other slipping between my legs. I felt his firm hand cup my pussy through my skirts, his fingers flexing, offering me just a tease of what was to come. He pulled me to my feet. My boots crunched into the snow. I tried to turn around to look at him, and he said, "No. Not yet." He growled, "The hunter has become the hunted."

"I can't hunt you now with these." I shook my wrists.

"Lucky for me." He pushed me against a tree, my body caught between the rough bark and his tall form. I knew that I was far away from my tutor Mr. Arrowen now. Agnar was a

98

wolf in heat, and nothing would stand between a wolf in heat and his mate.

Thank the gods.

"Lucky for *me*," I panted. "This is what I wanted all along. Rough...and hard..."

"Rough and hard?"

"Yes..."

The sound he made verged on a low howl. He took my hands in his and guided them around the trunk of the tree. The trunk was thick enough that my arms could only wrap partway around.

He pulled my hood off my hair and tugged the pins and combs that held my hairstyle in place. My locks tumbled down and he wrapped them around his hand, pulling my head back until my neck was craned. "Don't move."

I could see into his eyes, and I said nothing, but I smiled.

"And try not to look *so* pleased with yourself," he said sternly. But then he quickly kissed my mouth again. I was almost upside down as we kissed. He pushed my head against the tree again. Rough bark rubbed against my forehead.

The bodice of my dress laced around a stomacher, a flat piece of fabric that went in front to cover the corset. He slowly loosened the laces. Of course, I still had the stays on so I hardly felt looser at all; whalebone still held tight around my ribs. But I felt my bodice fall open around me, and he lifted my pale breasts out of my dress once again, holding their round weight in his palms.

"What luscious breasts you have," he said.

"Thank you, sir," I said, in my most proper accent.

He bent down. I couldn't quite see what he was doing, but when he stood up he was holding two snowballs, which he slapped right against my bare breasts.

I gasped. "You—!"

"Don't move, I said." He kissed me again, his body warm

and close behind me as my breasts were tortured with cold. "That's for the snowball fight."

"Ahh..."

He lowered his hands, although I saw him move more than I felt him. I was almost numb.

"And now you have the tightest little nipples I've ever seen." He lifted them up like he wanted me to look. I peered down and saw his hands twisting my nipples and I could barely feel it but *seeing* it made heat surge down through me and wetness bloom between my thighs. His chest slid down my back, his hands settling on my hips, and he leaned around me and sucked on my nipple. His warm mouth, I certainly felt, breathing life back into my frigid skin. My skin tingled all over as he warmed me again.

I grabbed his head, digging my fingers into his hair, and he immediately returned my hand back to the tree. "Patience, my little pupil..."

Wolves were not known for patience. He was not really an exception despite his words. His fingers yanked urgently at the ties and fasteners of my clothes, trying to figure out how to get them off.

"Bloody pain, isn't it?" I said. "And don't ask me. The maid handles all this."

"I think this is supposed to be part of the fun for humans," he grunted, ripping a lace. "But it's not made for wolves." He shoved my bodice off my shoulders, pulling my arms away from the tree. I didn't help him at all, but draped into his arms, relishing the feeling of the human clothes being pulled away.

"Don't rip 'em," I said. "Remember I still have to visit my grandmother."

He growled, tugging the skirt of my dress down over my hips, and then the petticoats. Underneath, I had just a light undergarment that barely covered my ass, my corset, and stockings. I could feel the cold air caressing my skin, and I burned so hot on the inside that it was more stimulating than anything.

Occasionally some sensible thought would scurry across my mind, telling me that a lady would not do something like this. I didn't really care. I was a wolf. I was happiest when I lived in the moment. Neither shame nor forethought were as powerful as instinct.

He pushed me back up against the tree with a slap to the ass.

"Oh! What was that for?" I asked.

"For having such a beautiful ass," he said, grinning. He stood behind me, now sliding his hands around my front and exploring my folds with his hand. I was soaking wet, more so by the moment. His hand met slickness and he milked the sensation with slow, deep strokes that drew a guttural sound out of my throat. One of his hands wrapped around my vocal chords like he wanted to *feel* that sound while his other hand plumbed my depths, his big thumb working up and down my clit while two—no, three—of his fingers found my entrance and started fucking me there with a strong, pulsing touch.

I growled at him. Speech was becoming meaningless. My fingernails scraped the bark of the tree, my nipples still rigid with cold, my breasts feeling heavy with numbness and yet also tingly. I pressed my head into his and licked his ear.

His teeth found the laces of my stays and tore at them as he kept touching me between the legs. It seemed to take forever for him to work the laces free, but finally, they fell away from my body and he pulled the final garment off of me. I was still wearing my cloak and my stockings and boots.

"And this," he said, "is for sucking my cock while you were supposed to be learning your letters."

"Ahh…" I could only make urgent sounds of encouragement.

He kept one hand inside me, hooked into my entrance while the other hand grabbed my thigh and pulled me back against his cock. When his hand withdrew, his stiff head was waiting to claim me, nudging me, stirring my wildness. He gripped me and thrust deep inside me, merciless and without any concern for how it felt for me.

"Ah!" I gasped now, and scraped my teeth against his cheek. His hands wrapped around me tight again, enfolding my arms with his, his fingers pushing against my cheek, turning my head to meet his mouth.

"I want to taste your screams," he said, thrusting deeper.

I did scream, and he muffled the scream with his tongue. I wasn't exactly in pain, though. It was relief. It was surrender to the most powerful half of my nature. I couldn't find any words, not of protest or encouragement. He was my mate and the master of my body. I needed him to take me until he was sated, until I was full of his seed, again and again until we had kits of our own. How my father and Katherine would have gasped to know what I really was, how easy it was for me to stop thinking about anything at all and surrender my will to the beat of nature that made bears hibernate and birds fly south and lemmings jump off cliffs and alley cats yowl.

That was all I was, in the end. All I wanted to be. To hunt and eat and sleep and fuck.

Right now, Agnar was exactly the same. He was gripping me tight, pressing me against the tree, his cock thrusting in and out of me so roughly that it was probably good my cloak covered some of me after all, or the tree bark might have scraped me up. "Ferrrsa..." My name rolled off his tongue, again and again, like it was the only word he remembered. His hands yanked on my nipples.

Lord, the brutality of it! It was such a release. After all those years of following orders in the work house, getting reprimanded, and slapped or locked up if I disobeyed. Of hunching over a tiny needle and denied the outdoors. And then, this new life—better in some ways, even worse in others. I had more to lose now, people to keep happy, and they all wanted me to be something I could never be. Even Agnar.

Until now. Nobody was thinking of the alphabet now, that was for fucking sure. Who'd been teaching who, then?

I was still moaning and growling against his hot breath, still tasting how sweet he was. He suddenly pulled at my jaw with his hand, his fingers in my mouth, tasting of my own cum. He bit my neck, pulling my cloak away from my nape. He thrust harder, and I was already aching. His cock lifted my feet right off the ground and his hands quickly caught my breasts again to support me. I leaned into his arms, the torturous rough caress, the relentless fucking. I loved every moment of it, the cold and the musk of our mingled scent and the grunting and the pain.

I started panting urgently as the orgasm swept over me. "Oh...oh...Agnar..."

"Fersa...yes...so wet..." Besides those few words, he barely even registered my reaction, except that it spurred him on. He didn't slow down at all.

By the time he started to come inside me, I felt thoroughly spent. His hot seed filled me, he slowed, and then he pulled back, breathing hard. I clung to the tree, feeling like my whole insides must be a giant bruise, but it was the kind of bruise that feels good, like I wanted to poke at it and feel it again.

He swept a hand around my waist and pulled me down into a snowbank beside him.

I rolled onto my side, so I finally had a really good look at him, naked beside me. I'm sure this would have been a startling sight to a lady. But to me, it suited him better than all those tight human clothes. I liked seeing his true self, a wild creature, ready to spring back into fur and claws at any moment. I loved seeing the lean muscle of his long arms and legs, the dark hair that lightly covered his arms and legs and thick chest, the pointless sort of hair that humans had, but I thought it still looked rather handsome.

"Now do you want my cloak?" I asked.

"Oh, I'm even less cold now than I was before."

"I'm a little cold..."

"Then you'd better keep it." Of course, it wasn't doing much good; my most sensitive bits were still exposed to the cold. He pulled me close to him so my head was on his shoulder, his hand stroking my hair idly. His golden eyes were framed by lashes that I realized were lighter than his hair.

"Your hair is really white, then?"

"Actually, almost more of a gray when it's hair and not fur," he said. "Silvery." He sighed, looking away from me. "But I've dyed it for a long, long time. And that must continue...especially now that I have more to lose."

He was starting to think now. I could see that. I didn't want him to think, not yet. How long could we go before we had to think about what had happened?

"Agnar," I said, stroking his chest. "Mm, I wish you could become a wolf and keep me warm right now, but then we couldn't talk."

"Do you want to talk?"

"No." I laughed.

"I shouldn't stay," he said. "You have somewhere to be." He shifted position, leaning one long arm forward to snatch up my clothes from where they had fallen in a crumpled pile, and started pulling the skirt up my legs.

He grabbed my stays and folded them around me, carefully tightening the laces. I felt like I was being put back together again—but in what form? A sort of pretty little marionette.

"Men's clothes are only a little better," he said. "If it's any consolation."

"I doubt that."

"My cravat feels like it's choking me."

I pulled up the straps of my bodice. The wool did feel nice and warm to my poor human self. "Where are your clothes?"

"I have a little spot in the rocks where I put them." He spun me around to look in my eyes. "Fersa," he said. "This is serious."

I shrugged. I didn't want to have a *talk*.

"I shouldn't have done that," he said.

"Yes, you should. You definitely should. It was all pent up. And I'm glad I was the lucky girl who got to unpent it." I grinned.

He couldn't help but grin back before it faded. "Was it rough and hard enough for you?"

"Maybe. It'll hurt to walk."

"Good. Every step will remind you of me."

My stomach growled. He perked up, so wolf-like in his expression that I could almost imagine his wolf ears moving forward. A wolfkin's mate was always very attuned to her needs. It was instinctual once mating occurred. I had forgotten about that but I saw it in him now, the protective nature I associated with men of my clan from childhood, and my cheeks warmed with affection.

"You're hungry," he said. "I'll hunt you something before you go."

I nodded. It warmed my heart to be taken care of like this.

He shifted easily, and I ran my hands through his fur one more time and kissed his forehead before he ran off. "Don't go far."

When he was gone, and I was left alone, I straightened

out my clothes and held my cloak around me. I started to shiver. I watched him disappear into the forest, his white fur blending in with the snowy landscape. My smile slowly faded, the warmth in my cheeks vanishing against a faint but biting breeze. The silver cuffs started feeling cold against my skin, even when I took my gloves out of my valise and tugged my sleeves down. Father had put them on to prevent me from the life of a wolf...

Or to protect me, I thought darkly.

Because it was easy to pretend my past wasn't quite real even as I mourned Mother every day. But here in the woods, I remembered how it really was. This was my home, and it also wasn't safe. Humans and elves feared wolves and took every excuse to destroy them.

No, Agnar is right. We really, really, really shouldn't have done that.

Chapter Fifteen

FERSA

WE HAD TO PART WAYS, of course. I had to move on. We shared a rabbit and by then the light of day was beginning to creep downward.

"Go see your grandmother," he said. "Spend these days with her, while the heat rises inside you and your restless thoughts race through you."

"You bastard." We kissed deeply. "I don't want to go. I feel much too wild to behave myself for an old lady."

He laughed. "I don't have much wealth to offer you, and certainly no good name. I think, if we're to have any future together, your father has to be able to tell himself that I'm the only man capable of taming you for society."

"Oh, I don't want to hear any of that boring *human* talk now," I griped, poking the snow with my stick.

"I can't be a cad in the eyes of the Rafferty clan," he said. "I must be a bore. Go on with you now." He pulled me to my feet and smacked my ass again.

I made a face, kissed him one more time, and started plodding down the path.

Even though my grandmother had made this unusual choice to live alone in the woods, I had a particular idea of old humans. Stooped, doddering, dowdy, old-fashioned... I didn't really expect her to be *fun*. Plus I was afraid of Patrick showing up.

I smelled woodsmoke before I saw the cabin, and I heard the whack of an axe before I saw the woman chopping up a huge fallen tree branch.

She was tall and only a little stooped, with white hair twisted in a thick coil of braids, sloppily pinned. Physical exertion had obviously warmed her up, because the sleeves of her blouse were rolled up. She wore a humble brown bodice and her skirt was a good foot off the ground so she could easily move in sturdy boots. She heard me coming from a fair distance and looked up, wiping her brow and planting a hand on one hip, the other perched on the handle of her axe.

I brightened a little. My grandmother was actually magnificent.

"Hello," she called. "You must be my granddaughter."

"Yes. I'm Fersa."

"I have soup waiting for you if you're hungry, and cakes for tea, but I hope you haven't gotten too spoiled there in town." Her accent was still very refined. "It is nice to have company for yule."

"No, ma'am." I laughed. "This is perfect."

"I was just working on a little clean up. This dratted branch came down in a recent ice storm and took out part of my hens' enclosure." She motioned to a chicken coop.

"Well, I'm happy to help around the land," I said.

"You're hardly dressed for it," she said, pacing around me with a scrutinizing expression.

I shrugged. "This is all Mrs. Rafferty offered me. I'm not sure she knows what work clothes actually look like."

"Yes, I know, that's what passes for country attire in town. And you do look lovely. But there's no one to see you out here...well, no one you ought to be messing with." She gave a stern look that made me nervous again. "Come in."

I entered the little house, which was mostly comprised of one room, but it had a smaller side lean-to that formed its own room, and a loft beneath the steeply pitched ceiling as well. "You'll be sleeping up there," she said. "The heat from the stove rises up near your bed and I do think you'll be quite cozy. Feel free to settle in while I get the kettle on."

I climbed the ladder with my valise and dumped it next to the bed, which was spread with a feather-stuffed quilt. There was a small table roughly made of branches and a crosscut piece of tree trunk, all with the bark still on them, topped with a simple glass vase holding some holly. Dried herbs hung from the rafters. A desk sat by the single small window. The panes were frosted with ice patterns. A rag rug covered the floor.

It was much more comfortable to me than the fine house I had left, although I could see it getting lonely.

Downstairs, she had set the table with an embroidered tablecloth, napkins and proper silverware and china cups, and set out a plate of golden-brown scones.

"I'm not much of a cook, I'm afraid," she said. "I had servants in my married days."

"You don't have to go to any of this bother for me," I said. *I just ate a freshly caught rabbit...*

"I try to always go to some trouble," she said. "Even for myself alone. I try to respect myself as my own guest, sitting down to a meal. Eccentric as it may sound, it's how I was raised. I can't bear the thought of forgetting my manners entirely." She put out a dish with sugars and then the tea. I was rather charmed by the whole thing. "I don't have milk," she added, apologetically. "I'll fetch some from the Donnell farm tomorrow."

"You don't have to; I don't mind."

"So, my dear," she said, sitting down. "Douglas's wolfkin girl, at long last. You don't look as wild as I expected."

"They've tried their best to make a lady out of me."

"How is that going? For you, I mean? On the outside, I can see they've done a good job."

"Oh, well..." I was conscious of having very disheveled hair. "It's all in the clothes. I'm—well—I might be a disappointment."

"A disappointment? I hardly think so! Douglas was so smitten with your mother, you would hardly believe. He and Katherine are very congenial, and certainly a much better match for having a life together. Wolves and humans make for terrible, terrible arrangements. But he was never *mad* about Katherine. Your mother gave him something a human girl would not have been able to give."

"What?" I was lapping up this gossip even more than the delicious tea.

"The chance to shed his rigid upbringing. I'm sure he told you how strict and cruel his grandfather was."

"Oh aye, it was practically the first thing he said."

"What are these on your wrists?" She suddenly noticed the silver cuffs. As I had my elbows on the table and the warm teacup between both hands, my sleeves had crept downward.

I looked down. "I turned into a wolf...at a ball. It was happening in the mornings, too. So these prevent that from happening."

"Ahh...you asked for them, or your father insisted?"

"They put them on for my own good after I fainted at the ball." I don't know why I was making excuses for it. I wanted the cuffs off, but I still couldn't believe I had lost control in front of all those people.

Grandmother tsked. "I guess it is for the best. We don't need any wolvenfolk sniffing around here. But I think I'll talk to Douglas about it. It's very easy to slip into controlling everything when you're the head of an estate."

"Thank you..." I liked her more by the moment and it was making me feel like opening up. "They've been very kind to me, by and large. I don't want to complain. I'm grateful. I just...can't help being what I am sometimes. The second I got there, it was corsets and hair ribbons and lessons in reading and writing and numbers... I'll never be good at any of that. There's so much to learn, and—I can't learn it. It's miserable to just sit there. I can't even take a walk without a chaperone, and when I tried, I got attacked by some bloody dock worker or something..."

"What kind of life do you want?" Grandmother asked. "Would you rather live in a wolf clan?"

"My clan is dead."

"I have some acquaintance with the clan in these woods. If it was what you *really* wanted, you might be able to join them. There are quite a few handsome young men in that clan, I daresay! But they range mostly westward. You wouldn't see your family here very often at all."

I frowned. No one had ever offered to let me back into a wolf clan before. The fact was, they weren't *my* clan. My father was my flesh and blood. John, Francis and Thomas were my brothers.

"I—I don't know. I would rather find a way to manage in town."

"Then, find a way. But town won't change for you. You'll either have to change town, or accept that many people will consider you an eccentric. Why do you think I live out here?"

"Why do you, exactly?"

"I needed to escape, like Douglas did. To know what it was to be free. But make no mistake, I'm a strange woman." She chuckled. "He was willing to go back there and be the man he needed to be, in order to claim the estate. I was never going to get more than a smidgen of inheritance. No expectations on an aging widow, is there? I decided I liked my independence. I'm not sure one choice is better than the other. I miss my old life more often than I'd like to admit, but I still have no regrets."

"I see…" I ventured, "The tutor Father hired to teach me my letters is a wolf."

"A *wolf* as a tutor?"

"He's a strange wolf."

"I'd imagine so!" She looked at me askance and urged another scone on me with a nudge of the plate. "You like this strange wolf, do you?"

"Yes. I do. Even though he pesters me about learning."

"What about Patrick Rafferty?"

"Oh…you've heard about that."

"He's been courting you? Yes. I've heard. Patrick comes to visit fairly often. He likes the forest."

"I'm not sure about Patrick…"

"I must say, I think he would be a good match for you. More acceptable for your family, as well, but I think you'd be happy too. Wolves don't make for good husbands."

"So everyone says, but—"

"You prefer this wolf, eh? Even though you don't want to learn your letters?"

"I'm not sure I could be happy with a human, but I think I could be happy with him. He understands what I am. I don't think I'd mind keeping his house and having his kits… He's not a man of means, it's true, but I don't care about that."

"But Fersa, you keep up with those lessons of yours. Learn to write and understand your household finances. Don't ever just marry a man and have his 'kits' when he has an education and you don't."

On one hand, I understood what she was trying to say. But it still made my stubbornness flare. "My mother didn't have an 'education'."

"She was a wolf, wasn't she?"

"And so am I!" I tapped my teaspoon on the table, restless. "I suppose it's all well and good to be ambitious and learned. But—it's not what *I* really care about. I don't need to write down the names of trees and flowers to know what they look like and taste like or what illnesses they're good for. My mother knew everything about the forest around her. She was a good huntress. And she was fun and playful. She seemed like the smartest woman I'd ever known, and the happiest too, and she still does. And now I feel like I'm not worth anything until I learn all these things...which I suppose means she was never worth anything." I swallowed down a lump in my throat.

"That's not true," Grandmother said, her voice gentle but still a little brisk. "But you're in a different world now."

"I *know* I am. Maybe I wouldn't mind if there wasn't so much pressure. I think I'd rather be the wife of a humble man than a rich one like Patrick, truly. I don't need to go to the fanciest parties in town. I want a husband who understand me, and I want children of my own. I want to teach them the things my mother taught me, and play with them at the edge of the forest...but at night, I want to tuck them into bed and know that no one will drive an arrow through my heart or theirs."

I started to cry in earnest. It welled up like a flash flood, no real warning. I had mourned my mother slowly and privately over the past several years, all while trying to adjust to life in the work house. I hated mourning her, I really did. I wanted to move on. The best way to honor my memories of her would be to have children of my own, and to love them as fiercely as she loved me. I didn't really want to shove my father away either. I wanted a *family*.

"It's all right, dear..." Grandmother patted my head. "It's not a bad thing at all to know what you really want. I just know that, in the human world, men have too much power already. Sometimes you think you know a man, and it turns out you don't. Don't give them any more than you must."

Later that evening, I opened the drawers of the desk in my bedroom and found paper and pen. I practiced the letters Agnar had taught me. I didn't always like my grandmother's advice, but I found her easy to respect, more like my mother than most humans I had met. Maybe the lines between humans and the wolvenfolk weren't as rigid as we assumed.

This, of course, came after a long evening of conversation over soup and later on, a mug of beer. I washed the dishes for her, happy to do menial labor instead of using my brain. Whatever she said, I was much better suited to that! Maybe I should have been a housemaid instead of a wealthy man's daughter.

In the morning, she loaned me a plain work dress and I helped her finish chopping the branch into pieces, hauling it away from the broken fence. We mended it together. Soon, my hands were dirty, my hair was tied back in a kerchief, and my shiny new boots were caked with slushy muck.

Grandmother still stopped for a proper lunch with a properly set table and proper china, though. It seemed to be her one rule, that no matter what, a woman should keep a tidy house and table. I didn't really care, but I found myself admiring her dedication to it.

The sun set early and we did some baking for yule.

"I'll bring some sweets to the Donnells," she said the next

morning. "They don't have a woman in the house, just little Eliza and she can hardly bake a biscuit."

"I could come with you."

"No, no," she said. "You stay here. I have some boring business to attend to over there. Feel free to take a nap or use my sewing basket or anything else you like."

"Boring business?"

"We might trade some chickens," she said.

I had a vague sense of suspicion, but I told myself that I should certainly be able to trust my grandmother, and the sense quickly disappeared when several *mostly* pleasant days of work and conversation passed. I can only say mostly, because I was coming into full heat and everything was tinged with the torture of wanting to mate. I think it was only improved by the fact that I had actually gotten to mate for once. Sometimes I thought I caught Agnar's scent on the wind. I think he was watching me, and I was always looking for him. One day I took a walk and passed the tree where we had made love. There was a cluster of snowdrop flowers tucked into a crook between the branches.

Be careful, my dearest...

And then, I was outside feeding the hens one morning when I saw Patrick riding down the woodland path. With the trees bare, he was visible at a far distance.

"Good morning, Miss Fersa!" he called as he came closer.

"Good morning," I said, straightening up. I was a bit dirty, not that I cared about impressing him.

Grandmother came out of the house. "Patrick Rafferty, you rascal." She kissed his cheek. "You got my letter?"

"Yes, indeed, but I was already thinking about coming out." He looked at me. "The white wolf has been spotted around these parts."

My entire body was tensing up. "Well, I'm afraid I can't help you. My father's cuffed me with silver and I can't shift.

My nose is hardly better than a human now, and I'm no hunter without teeth and claws."

He whipped something out of his pocket and tossed it to me. "The key to your chains, my lady."

Oh no, I thought, as I caught the object that glinted by me. "Father gave this to you? He didn't want me to hunt!"

"I *might* have nicked it while paying a visit," he said. "But you don't think it's fair that he cuffed you, do you? It's not right. I don't care what happened at the ball, Fersa—I swear I don't."

I felt panic sweep over me. One bad thing about being wolvenfolk is that I was easily inclined to panic. When you're an animal, you must be ready to run at the first sign of danger. I didn't know what to say now, so my feet carried me right back into house, almost without knowing it.

I clutched the table. *Oh no. Oh no. They've spotted Agnar because he was out here looking for me. I can't hunt him. But what do I say?*

Grandmother stepped in to the cabin. "Now, dear, I know what you're thinking. But I think you should at least give Patrick one chance to impress you. It wouldn't hurt to hunt with him. Aren't you itching to run? I can see how restless you are."

"I can't hunt," I said.

"Why not? You don't want the reward?"

"Not for a fellow wolf..."

"His own clan wants him dead!"

I felt like I was going to be sick. I couldn't hunt Agnar. I wouldn't even take the risk of agreeing to hunt him just to warn him, because my presence might lure Agnar out and then it would be too late.

Take your time and think about it a moment. I took a deep breath. I just needed a reasonable excuse. I clutched the cuffs at my wrists. "Grandmother, you know I've made my choice.

I want to live in Pennarick, as a human. I don't want to hunt as a wolf, and certainly not with Patrick. This isn't an easy choice, but nevertheless, it's the better one, and I don't want to tempt myself to trouble."

"I see, I see," she said. "I would have liked you to share that reward, but Patrick might be able to take care of it on his own. I'll feel much better walking these woods without some rogue wolf on the loose."

What could I do?

Patrick joined us for dinner. The entire meal was a blur of terror as I listened to him discuss his plans.

If only I could get some sort of message to Agnar that Patrick was staying with the Donnells up on the hill and that he and Farmer Donnell planned to set out Sunday morning from the ridge. I knew everything now and I couldn't write. But maybe it didn't matter. I would be afraid to leave out evidence that I was on the white wolf's side.

Why did I have to be attracted to the one wolf who had committed a terrible crime and had no allies, even in his own clan?

Chapter Sixteen

AGNAR

FROM THE SHADOWS, I watched Fersa's grandmother light the candles.

I should go back to town. I knew this. But I couldn't. The driving force of desire for my mate kept me close to her at all times. I wanted to protect her, even knowing I never could. This was always my most vulnerable time of year, when I could no longer fight what I was. Now, it had become impossible.

So I stayed hidden, and I watched the door close on her and Patrick Rafferty. I smelled the traces of other wolves on the wind. My old clan didn't usually range this close to human settlements. But I was not alone in this forest. They must be hunting me too.

At least let me say goodbye before I'm caught...

Patrick walked out of the house with a lantern in his hand, and got on his horse to ride off into the snowy night.

Good. Leave her alone. I slept there, my head on my paws, watching the candle go out upstairs, where Fersa slept.

In the morning, after breakfast, her grandmother also left. Fersa stood outside, watching her go. She was more beautiful than ever in the clothing of a peasant, her hair in a disheveled braid, her skirts hanging around her lean body without the cage of her undergarments, her red cloak bright against the snow. She went into the stable and I seized my chance. I shifted into a man, threw on my shirt and trousers, and crept in out of the forest. I would surprise her when she walked in the door.

The cottage was a cozy space and it smelled of her. I wished more than ever that things had been different. That I could give her a home.

The table and two chairs were positioned by the wood-stove, which was warm. Freshly baked scones were on the table. Her grandmother's bed was against the far wall. I was considering helping myself to a scone when she walked in and her eyes flew open.

"You shouldn't be here!"

"I know."

"I'm serious! They're hunting you! Grandmother went over to talk to Patrick just now!"

"She'll be gone for a while then."

"She said she would," Fersa admitted. "She got up early to bake, and told me to make my own lunch..."

"I can't stay away," I said. "Fersa...you're my mate now. Everything in me is screaming to be near you. I've resisted my true nature for fifteen years. And all it's given me is a life of loneliness. You're right. Learning only goes so far..."

"Don't say that!" She flew right onto my lap, her cloak fluttering behind her, and threw her arms around my neck. "Please...you have to keep resisting. I'm sorry I tried to convince you otherwise. I need you to be human—and stay safe. Please—go!"

I clutched her body. What I felt for her was more than mere lust—it was raw need, insistent as having to eat or sleep. "I don't know if I can."

Her eyes melted into mine. "I know. I feel it too. Aren't we silly? Our kind can think like humans but we still have to act like animals."

"Just in case I'm caught, I had to see you one last time."

I felt her quickening breath as my hands spread on her back. Now there was nothing between her skin and mine but a layer of wool and another of linen. She felt soft and strong at once. "I need you one last time...," I said. "You've done this to me, Fersa. I managed just fine before you came along."

"Agnar..." She pressed her face against mine and opened her mouth. Her tongue lolled slightly like a panting wolf. She looked like I'd already fucked her. How could I not when she looked like that? I filled that mouth with my own. My hands slid down to her ass, digging into her flesh. I couldn't get enough of the way it felt to hold her taut form. A wolf couldn't get his hands on a woman like this, but as a wolf I could smell every nuance of her scent. I looked forward to having her every way I could.

"Fersa...," I growled.

She kissed me again, fixed me with a look, and then she stood up and unfastened buttons at the back of her dress. I watched, rapping my nails on the table.

Gods, I hated myself sometimes. I hated that I would never have the discipline of a human. But I had also worked so hard to deny that, and I had never known as much happiness as I did with her. I was unraveling, grabbing her body before she had finished undressing.

"Oh!" she cried, surprised as I scooped her into my arms

and threw her onto the bed, tearing her dress off over her head.

Now I growled low, digging my hands into her hair. "This is what you've done to me, Fersa. Fifteen years of control, fifteen years of manners and letters out the damn window. You meant to tear apart my facade. You knew what you were doing to me. The least you deserve is for me to fuck you until you can't walk at all."

I quickly unfastened my buttons, shoved her legs apart, and thrust into her, giving her my full strength. Her back arched, lifting her breasts to me, her arms collapsed on the bed with her palms open and her fingers falling open, showing me every creamy inch of her bare skin: her arms, the hollow of her throat, the little indent of her navel between the soft curves of her hip bones. I laced my hands with hers, using my palms as leverage to pound into her. Her inner walls clenched around my cock. "Patrick Rafferty could never fuck you like this."

"I know it!" she gasped. "I don't want him! I tore apart your—your facade—" I'm not sure she knew the word— "because I needed you. I just didn't know you were the white wolf. Please, don't be caught! I can't lose you too. Stop...stop. We have to do this properly...ask Father for...my hand." She trailed off into heavy panting. "Don't mess up my grandmother's bedspread."

I shut my eyes, feeling her slip away even as she was so close to me. "If I want to be your husband, I will never be able to change into a wolf again," I said. "I can never take the risk."

"Agnar..." Her voice was thick. "Then I won't either. Lock the cuffs around my wrists. We'll be humans together forever. Just don't leave me."

Chapter Seventeen

FERSA

HE DIDN'T SAY ANYTHING, but he picked me up and laid me down on the rug. It was a lot less comfortable than the bed, but I didn't really care. My life had not been remarkable for its comforts. I shoved his jacket off his shoulders so I could see his fine body, but before I could get any farther, his hands laced with mine and he claimed me again and again with a strength that made me shiver with delight. The primal beauty of him, the complete lack of control unleashed... I wondered how he had ever held back. That made him all the more intriguing to me, that he could possibly have posed as a scholar and tutored other bored young women without doing this to them—that I had been the one to remind him what he really was.

I was pretty much lost to sense at this point. His sharp teeth nipped at my neck and then his tongue raked up my skin, anywhere he could bite and taste me, as he made little growling sounds of desire that drove me insane. My moans were a begging response. No matter how deep he went, it was never deep enough, but the strong and steady motion of his cock—sliding out, then slamming back into my slick folds— was slowly driving me closer and closer to the abyss. I was seeing stars, riding a wave of increasing, delicious sensation.

"Do you mean it?" he grunted. "Is that really want you want? You and me, human forever?"

My eyes were filled with tears, I realized. "I want you."

"Who will teach our children to be wolves?"

"I—I don't know. I don't want to think about it. I just want you."

"You *have* to think about it. It's important."

"It'll be hard," I finally said. "I don't know. But we have to try. You're my mate and—I don't think anyone else would ever do. I love my father...my little brothers. I will miss the forest forever, but I don't want to live there."

"Ahh...Fersa...I'll try to do it properly then. Will you marry me?"

"Yes, yes!"

"By day, we can dress up and pretend to be humans...and at night..." He made a satisfied sound deep in his throat, and held me close, my bare skin pressed against the buttons of his shirt. I dug my fingers in his shoulders, crying out as another deep thrust of his rigid manhood brought me to my peak again. I felt like a mess of sprawled limbs and disheveled hair, my body alight with tingling nerves and pulsing inner muscles.

It was only after the last tremblings of my orgasm that I started to realize just how hard the floor was, and how exhausted I was. I panted. "Please..."

"Not yet," he said. "We fuck like wolves now. Joined until I come inside you. I will teach you different lessons now...like how to please me."

I knew precisely what he meant, although I had never

been able to mate in a wolf form of course. Wolves locked together when they mated, the male becoming engorged as the female tightened around him, unable to break apart until they were done.

"I think I knew that lesson before you did."

"Maybe you're right..."

He kept stroking my sensitive body, my skin burning like fire against him. I squirmed. A part of me didn't want to surrender control even though I grew more aroused the more he ordered me.

And then, as I felt him release inside me once again, something in me broke open and relaxed. I melted like a puddle of wax.

He's so beautiful.

Day by day, I was beginning to appreciate both sides of his nature: one controlled and bookish, the other wild and intuitive. Maybe I was beginning to appreciate both these things in my own blood too. I saw all of this in him, every moment, and it seemed like magic to me. I treasured every bit of him, how his eyes were alert and intelligent, and his hair somewhat groomed and yet not anything like the other men in town, and the strong forearms against the pale clean cotton of his shirt. I kept touching him like I was discovering the shape of a person for the first time.

He had slumped beside me, stroking my hair in a similar way. "Can you walk?" he asked, with a low laugh.

"I wish I didn't have to," I said. "You know, I think I can make Father understand. I'm sure he'll give me trouble, but I also think he likes you. Sometimes he says things...like he knows that I will never truly adjust to his life."

"Aye, I think so too." He kissed my nose. "I think he wants you to be happy."

I was grinning like a fool as we finally forced our bodies apart and got our clothes back in order. Agnar fastened my buttons, one by one, and tied my apron around my waist, as if he wanted any excuse for his hands to linger on my body. He wrapped his arms around me from behind.

"I'm already ready to have you again."

"I can tell. But maybe we'd better have something to eat before I have to send you off. We don't want my grandmother to catch you, now do we? I don't think it would be the best way to present you to the family."

"You're right." He pulled out a chair, still holding my apron strings in one hand. He tugged me down onto his lap. "Still, no need to part ways yet, aye?"

I handed him a scone and took one for myself. I was half-starved after all that and grandmother's scones were flaky with butter, flecked with dried fruits. We had our fill of them in no time at all, and it was only afterwards that I realized just how many crumbs we'd scattered everywhere.

"I'd better sweep! Grandmother keeps a very clean table..." I stood up, but my stomach was feeling strange. I grabbed the back of the empty chair and sat down.

"You feel it, too?" Agnar asked. "What's in those scones?"

"Nothing! She makes them every day! She got the butter from the Donnell farm the other day, but—I don't think—"

I felt as if my stomach was stuffed with rocks. Agnar turned a sickly color, and then he pounded his fist on the table. "Did you tell her about me?" he said.

"I told her my tutor is a wolf, and that I have some interest in you. But she doesn't know you're the white wolf. Still, you weren't exactly careful, were you?" Panic rose within me. "Would she poison me too?"

"It's not fatal, I'm sure. King Brennus wants me alive..."

This didn't feel like bad food, which I had endured plenty often in the work house. I felt a heaviness in my stomach, and I could barely get out of my chair.

"This feels like magic," I said. "Can you escape?"

He struggled to get to his feet. He was breaking into a sweat. "I'm sure I can't change. It feels like a weight is dragging me down."

"Grandmother..." My head sank into my hands. She must have betrayed me, but I still didn't understand how she had known.

We were both trapped in the cabin, hardly able to leave our chairs, and before long we heard Patrick's horse approaching.

"Hide!" I told him. "Under the bed, maybe?"

"It's no use, Fersa," he said. "It's time to face my fate, then. I'm sorry."

"No—no!" The door opened, and Grandmother and Patrick had barely set foot in the door when I cried, "You can't take him from me! I already lost my mother! He's not a criminal!"

"Are you sure about that?" Grandmother said, arching a brow.

And they weren't alone. A brown wolf came right into the house and sniffed Agnar. Agnar glared at the wolf. The wolf looked back at my grandmother and it seemed as if he nodded.

"Wait! Do you know this wolf? What's happening?" I was starting to feel cornered. I dug the silver key out of my pocket. My instinct was to change into a wolf myself—and hide. I couldn't do that, of course.

Patrick sighed. "Little Red, my sweet, I—"

"I'm not your sweet!"

He stiffened. "Fersa—"

"I never wanted to hunt my own kind! I don't want to be tamed!"

"Patrick, don't lay it on too thick now," Grandmother said. "And Fersa, calm yourself down. I don't know what this man told you and why you've decided to trust him, but...you know he's the third Longtooth brother, don't you?"

"What of it?"

"What of it?" Grandmother repeated. "You know what he's guilty of! It's no small thing! Did you really think you could hide it? When you first came here, I saw the white fur all over the back of your dress."

"Fucking hell!" I screamed.

Grandmother almost smiled, but then she saw Agnar and the smile disappeared. He was sitting at the table, relatively calm, his hands laced. "So you knew all along. You guessed I would visit and the scones were a trap."

"Yes," Grandmother said. "They're enchanted. As soon as you eat them, they turn to magical stones in your stomach— for a day. Long enough to slow you down, but it won't kill you."

Agnar said, "There is nothing I can say to change what I did, but...I killed one blue stag, fifteen years ago. I was a young man, and it was the price asked by the man who agreed to give me an education. I knew it was wrong, but I didn't realize how wrong. I've paid for it ever since. I've never been able to return to my own clan. And as for my brothers, the last time I saw them, Ergar was eight. Garrin was six."

"You'll have to tell that to King Brennus," Grandmother said, more gently.

The wolf beside her suddenly changed into a man. "Don't look at me like that, woman, it's nothing ye ain't seen before," he told her as he raised himself on two bare legs.

Grandmother crossed her arms. "*Please*," she said.

"Agnar Longtooth," the wolf said. "I'm the alpha of the Endless Firs clan in these woods. Along with the other nine clans of Mardoon, I've made a pact with King Brennus, to find ye and bring ye to him. And in exchange, no wolf will ever be bothering with academies and books and all this trouble you've gotten yourself into."

My stubborn nature immediately bristled. "Wait a minute! Why? Does that mean I can't learn to read anymore?"

"Yer half human," he said, a bit dismissively. "The new law applies to pure bloods. First it was this one, and then it was Ergar, and the last thing we need are rogue wolves raping and killing. It puts us all in danger! It gives them an excuse to kill *us*!"

"I understand," Agnar said, solemn and strangely accepting.

"No!" I cried. "Please! I don't know about Ergar, but Agnar doesn't deserve—whatever King Brennus would do to him!"

"I am sorry," Grandmother said. "I truly am. But Fersa, he's the king." She suddenly clenched the wolf's arm. "Maybe —she should go with him and plead the man's case. From what I've heard, he really doesn't seem like a harm to anyone."

"We don't need other wolves wanting that kind of learnin'. We'd rather no one plead his case."

"But—Fendor—do you remember when I showed you around my little homestead?"

"You showed me how to use yer tools and things," he grumbled. "That's different."

"Is it? You told me the gardens saved you all from starvation in that one bad winter. I only knew most of that from my own reading. I didn't grow up on a farm. Maybe it's not a bad thing if, once in a while, a wolf feels a pull to learn the things humans know. They could come back and help all of you—if you made them welcome."

"Well, it's hardly up to me, is it, woman? You'd have to talk to the other nine clans," Fendor said, glowering. "And that doesn't fix the fact that Brennus has a hefty price on his head."

"I *will* go with him," I said. "What do you think—Brennus will do to him?"

"Don't know," Fendor said. "The elven kings aren't as brutal as they used to be. I expect he might get away with a whipping and prison."

"A slow death sentence rather than a quick one!" From what I'd heard, life in prison was hardly worth living.

Agnar bore all this with a stoic expression, but he didn't look at me. "Fersa, don't put yourself in danger on my account."

"You think I could just prance on home and not even know what happened to you? Ridiculous."

"C'mon, daylight's a wastin'," Fendor said.

Patrick took out another set of cuffs and collar for Agnar, sized for a man's wrist and neck. He handed them to Fendor without a word, and then he grabbed my arm. "Can I talk to you a moment?"

"Don't grab me!"

"All right, all right. But can I talk to you outside?"

"I guess."

We stepped outside. "Fersa...do you think it's really true, what he's saying?"

"What?"

"That he was young when he killed the stag. I know he's your tutor. He doesn't seem like a criminal, I'll admit."

"He's not!" I snapped.

"Why didn't you tell me when I asked if you wanted to *hunt* him?"

"What was I supposed to say?"

He scratched his head. "That you didn't want to hunt your own kind...?"

I hugged myself. "I couldn't have told you, Patrick. You would've been jealous. You would've hurt him."

"Lord, what kind of a man do you take me for, Fersa? I'll admit, I'm not well pleased to find that you had your eye on another man this whole time while I was courting you, but I wouldn't force you to marry me. And I wouldn't send an innocent man to prison. Your grandmother was worried; she thought maybe this wolf was bribing you to feed him or worse."

"I—" My mouth hung open a moment. I had never thought I could trust him. "I was so sure everyone would be furious at me if I told the truth."

"I doubt your father will be pleased either, but in the end it's still better to tell the truth. He wouldn't cut you off for marrying your tutor, I'm sure of that."

"Oh..." I covered my mouth. "Then...I've made a terrible mistake... Patrick. I'm sorry."

"It's all right. Here." He handed me a handkerchief although I wasn't crying yet.

"I never expected you to be...nice."

He raised his brows. "I wasn't being nice already? After I saved you out there on the docks and everything else?"

"You said you wanted to tame me..."

"I was trying to flirt. I didn't think you'd want me to mince words about—you know—bedroom matters. I suppose it's for the best, because you have my head spun around at this point."

I dared to reach for his hand. "I have a hard time trusting anyone outside of my own kind. The elves killed my clan, you know. I feel as if my father and Katherine must disapprove of everything I do, even when they're trying to be nice. But maybe...I have it all wrong."

"I think you do," he said. "They love you. And I would never wish you any misery either. I don't think any Rafferty would. Unfortunately, I don't know what to do about Mr. Arrowen. He's wanted far and wide and a few innocent white wolves have been killed in looking for him, so Fendor certainly isn't going to let him off."

"I—I see," I said, finally making use of the handkerchief. "I guess I should have known that it's my lot to lose the ones I love, over and over..." I started making choked sounds, but I forced myself to keep it together. "But I am going with him."

"I'll go too, if you like," Patrick said. "I'll vouch for him as a citizen of Pennarick."

"Thank you. Truly."

He patted my head. "I guess I'll just be calling you 'cousin'." He sighed and reached for the doorknob.

"Wait—can I ask you one more thing?"

"Of course."

"Did Fendor and my grandmother—I mean—how do *they* know each other?"

He chuckled. "I don't think it's my place to offer details, because she's not much for giving them, but to be sure, if you ask her about having a relationship with a wolf she has a lot of opinions on the matter, most of them rather feisty. I know that, because I asked her about you. She said you're likely to be easily distracted, half-wild, and frustrating beyond words —but also, hard to get rid of once your loyalties are set." He smirked. "I guess that's why he keeps coming around, eh?"

Chapter Eighteen

AGNAR

THE RIDE to Mardoon was a long and sobering one. It was difficult to ponder that my life might be, in essence, over, even as I was beside the girl I had hoped to have a future with.

Fendor drove the cart with Patrick watching over the proceedings—I still wasn't especially fond of him, but I had to admit he kept the proper distance from Fersa now—while Fersa and I sat on the bench in back. The weather was fine and it took just a few days to reach the castle of Arindora, where King Brennus and Queen Bethany held court. The humans of Pennarick quickly disappeared, replaced by the wood elves who made up most of the population. They dressed simply and were all rather rugged with cheerful country accents, even in the court itself.

In all my years, I had never gone to the capital, and normally I would have been more interested. It was hard to think of such things now. Absurdly, my telescope stuck out in

my mind. I had saved my coins for a long time to buy a telescope of my own. Now I might never look at the sky again.

"Presenting Fendor, leader of the Endless Firs wolf clan."

I wished I could better appreciate this view of the inside
of one of the great halls. I had never seen such a place before
and I knew the walls, paneled in wood, were covered in
centuries-old artwork of flora and fauna and the tapestries
and armor on display were all historic. I dared to glance up
and saw the scene of a wolf hunt, and decided it was well and
good not to pay attention.

King Brennus sat on his throne, a well-built man with
red hair and a restless look about him. Queen Bethany
seemed small and patient beside him, but her eyes were
appraising. She was rather scandalously known as an author
of novels and I wondered if my situation would be immor-
talized.

"Greetings," Brennus said. "I know what you've come for,
but I don't see any white haired wolfkin among ye. Please tell
me we're to have an end to all this mess."

"Aye, your majesty." Fendor bowed slightly, doffing a
battered straw hat. Fersa's grandmother had produced clothes
for him. "This fellow is the man you seek. Agnar Longtooth,
yon white wolf."

Bethany leaned forward, squinting at me. "Him?"

"It's true," I said. "But—"

"You have black hair."

"I dyed it."

Some courtiers murmured. This seemed to add an extra
note of scandal—a *disguise*.

"I killed a blue stag when I was fifteen years old," I said.
"I know that is no excuse for the crime. I would give anything
to turn the clock back and stop myself from doing it."

"You are very well spoken for a wolf," the queen said.
"Come a little closer?"

"Are y'getting near sighted, my dear?" Brennus said. "I tell you, too much reading will do it."

I took a step closer to the queen and Brennus suddenly barked at me, "Your brothers were villains if I've ever met one! They killed my man and they were about to do unspeakable things to my wife. What do you say to that?"

A sense of sudden despair washed over me, paired with a need to know answers to questions I shouldn't ask. "Tell me—what happened to them."

"Brennus and I were...staying in a cabin together, for our honeymoon," Queen Bethany said, a bit primly. "He had stepped out and your brothers came along. They tied me up with a rope and marched me out to a cabin in the woods. They spoke to me very crudely. I saved myself by promising to make them magic applesauce, but before long they grew impatient and they said they were going to rape me and eat me. I am not convinced they wouldn't have done it, if Brennus hadn't come in time. You don't seem a thing like them, I will say that."

"I—I haven't seen them since they were children."

Queen Bethany said, a little more softly, "Your brother, Ergar, said he wanted to attend the academy and have an education. They allowed him in. But he was...teased, by the other children, and he lost control. I think it was a very unfortunate situation. He seemed very angry at the world. And in pain..."

I believed her. I wished I didn't.

I shut my eyes briefly. I was afraid to say anything else. I didn't want to show emotion here. "Thank you for telling me, your majesty."

I tried not to look at Fersa. I was afraid she might blurt out something and make more trouble for me. I could feel her just beside me shifting her weight, trembling with indignation.

"What are we to do with him?" Brennus asked. "He has admitted his crime."

"His crime was wanting to know about the moon and stars," Fersa said.

I cringed. It just sounded stupid now. I was cursed with the bad decisions of my fifteen year old self.

"He's been an upstanding fellow in our town," Patrick said. "He's been working as a tutor and by all accounts, no one's had the least bit of trouble with him. I've heard he is patient and good with the children, even young Robert Powers who's had consumption and by all reports is a sour little boy. I've encountered the man many times and seen him display good manners and friendly conduct."

Fendor scoffed. "Some wolf he is. Your majesty, if you please. None of the clans want anything to do with this. Wolves ain't meant for learning. Does funny things to our heads, as you can see. I'd guess he might be a half-human or elf bastard, in which case you can weigh his human half. We have already decided our punishment: banishment, plain and simple."

"Hmm," Queen Bethany said. "Is that true? Is there any chance your father was a human or elf?"

"Oh, what does it matter, lass," Brennus said. "Either way, we've just got to address what he did and appease the forest, so we can be done with it."

"I would like to talk to him alone. Give the men their gold and send them on their way," Queen Bethany said.

Brennus looked bemused by his wife's order. "She's probably going to make a book out of you," he told me.

While I'm locked up in prison?

A man ushered Fendor out. "I want to stay! Please!" Fersa cried, but Patrick put an arm around her shoulders and said, "Let them speak." Damn the man, he was still thinking of swooping in on her.

"There isn't much I can say anymore," I said stiffly. "But I do think it's bad form to write a book about a man who can't tell his side of the story."

"Mr. Longtooth—"

"Mr. Arrowen, please," I said, although I was probably pushing my luck.

"Do you know a man named Alvo Giardi?" Queen Bethany asked.

"He was my first teacher," I said, glancing around. Was he here? And if so, would it be in my defense, or would it be the final blow?

"After what happened with your brothers, I couldn't stop thinking about the story Ergar told me. As terrifying as he was, his story haunted me. I wanted to write a happier ending for him, even if only in fiction, but first I've been doing some research on the wolvenfolk. I have a book I think you ought to see." She held out a leather-bound tome.

Taming the Wolf: An Account of Experiments in Educating and Civilizing the Boy-Child, Agnar of the Wolf Clans, by Alvo Giardi.

I opened the book with a sense of rising betrayal. I already knew what would be inside.

"I should have destroyed them," I said in a whisper.

He had taken all of the notes and turned them into a narrative, the story of how he, the wise intellectual Alvo Giardi, had attempted to "bestow the benefits of civilization" upon me, and how I had continually failed to truly appreciate them. All of my struggles, my tempers and my stupid questions were written down and twisted so that I seemed like a primitive creature who could never hope to match the wisdom of my munificent benefactor. And yet, the reader would surely cheer when I did finally grasp some new concept, after all the pages detailing Alvo's hopelessness that I ever would.

"He's the wolf child in the book?" Brennus asked.

"Yes," Bethany said. "You are, aren't you?"

"This—*bastard*," I said, leaving out a few words I dared not say in front of royalty. "He's the one who told me to kill the blue stag in the first place. He seemed like he wanted to help me, and all along he wanted to write a book."

"Mm," Bethany said. "It really isn't a very nice thing for an author to do. And it was a bestseller back in Lainsland, and on the continent! Clearly people are hungry for this sort of story..."

"Oh, I don't know about where this is all going," Brennus muttered.

"We could write a *rebuttal*," Queen Bethany said, her eyes lighting up.

"A rebuttal?"

"The *real* story. After all, my lord, you said I should stick to writing true stories from now on," Bethany told the king.

"The forest wants his head, lass. The trees told me, all the Longtooth brothers must be dead."

"Where did the name 'Arrowen' come from?" Bethany asked.

I almost smiled. That was a fond memory. "It came from a woman I taught to read," I said. "She was my mother's age, a widow who needed a boarder to pay her rent after her husband and son had been taken by the black fever. She'd always wanted to learn but she came from a farming family and no one taught her, nor would her husband take the time. I was happy to do it. We became friends, I should say, and she knew that I didn't want to use the name I was given. She told me to take hers, since her son would not have it any longer."

"Well, there we have it!" Bethany said. "You must officially give him a new name. He can't be a Longtooth anymore, he will have to be an Arrowen."

"I don't know, lass..."

"You tell me that the king of the wood elves can't give a man a new name and smooth things over with the forest?"

"And then what?"

"Well, we'll write the bestseller, and then..." She patted her stomach. "We'll need a patient tutor who is good with children. A fair penance, I'd say."

"Lass, you get me in more trouble by the day," King Brennus said.

"Don't pretend to be surprised." The queen smiled at him and then motioned to one of the attendants. "Show Mr. Arrowen to that little upstairs room overlooking the garden."

CHAPTER

FERSA

FENDOR WAS STILL COMPLAINING about wolves who "step outside their station" and I finally couldn't stand it anymore.

"Be quiet or I'll bite you! You don't dare bite me back either!"

Patrick held me back. "Fersa, I know you're upset—"

"*Upset?*"

"It'll be all right... Maybe his sentence won't be forever, and you've still got your family."

"Don't try to make things better when you can only make them worse!"

The door of the great hall flung open, and Agnar walked out. He looked at me. A guard was standing next to him. I couldn't bear it. "Don't—" I wiped away a tear. "What if I'm already pregnant?"

Agnar flew toward me, pulled me against him, and gave

me a stunning kiss. I didn't respond at first because it was the last thing I expected.

"I hope so," he said. "Because...I think everything's all right." He cupped my face between his hands and half-kissed, half-nipped my face a few times.

"What? What do you mean?"

"The queen has offered me a place here. Come on."

"Fersa?" I heard Patrick call behind me, as Agnar gripped my hand. "Are you coming back to Pennarick?"

"I—I don't know. I'll be back in a moment!" I had to walk fast to keep up with Agnar.

"I'm sorry. I'm relieved, that's all. I've been carrying around this terrible thing for so long." He paused. "And my brothers— Well, I'm just glad I won't let *you* down."

"We're living here? What about my family?"

Some of his excitement slid away. "It's only a few days' travel to visit."

"Maybe Katherine is better taken in smaller doses anyway." I brightened. "And elf women don't wear corsets! But...Father was so excited to have me nearby."

"I also didn't consider that maybe you don't have the best opinion of elves."

"Nah, it's the high elves I don't care for," I said, as we followed the guard up the stairs. I didn't even know where we were going. "It's all just very unexpected."

The guard showed us into a little room, a sort of drafty attic spot with a bed, a little table with two chairs and a writing desk, and a hearth with a few cooking implements. A window looked out over a beautiful garden.

"Your room, sir," the guard said. He bowed a little and left us alone to explore it, what little of it there was.

Agnar looked at me. "It's not Meadow Lost Manor."

"It's not even Grandmother's cabin."

"No. It's not. It's just...the only place I have now, I think."

"One prison for another, and another, and another..." I walked to the window. "But that is a much better garden."

"Fersa...if you don't want—"

I stopped and put a finger over his lips. "No, my love. I told you I would wear silver bands for you, if that's what I had to do. I would be human for you. The wolf in me knew from the start that you were mine, but it's the human in me that will keep you."

He crouched on one knee and took my hand. "Then, what human there is in me will ask if you'll be Mrs. Agnar Arrowen. I shall buy you a ring."

"Yes, Agnar. I will! On one condition."

"What is that?

"That Agnar Longtooth will fuck me on that bed right now because it's been a long ride in that cart."

He took my wrist and tugged me close enough that he could sweep an arm around me. "Aye, my love. As rough and hard as you please."

Epilogue

AGNAR

THE FOREST IS the place of mystery, the place where mortals vanish. When we die in the forest, our bones are quickly covered by moss and leaves and eaten by those that still live, and soon we are gone. But forests have long memories, too. I didn't know if I would ever be forgiven. Brennus named me Agnar Arrowen, and he spoke to the forest with his wife's scheme in mind, and the best he could do was a promise to keep me locked in his castle, never to set a single foot in the forest again.

It was a bitter sentence for a wolf, even a strange wolf.

Within a year, Fersa had borne two kits, one black-haired boy and one silver-haired girl, named Ergar—the name of my father as well as my brother—and Remma, after her mother. They both had a tendency to shift into wolves and howl all night long. We had to cuff them much of the time until they were old enough to understand, for the sake of the neighbors and to protect other babies and easily alarmed elves. Fersa sobbed while my heart broke in silence, although she was able to take them into the woods here and there—without me. Queen Bethany had a red-headed boy who was very advanced for his age, but terrified of my babes when they shifted into wolves, and also terrified of most everything else.

"Forget letters! You'll have to teach him to be brave!" she said. "He's going to be king someday."

I was looking forward to that. I think wolves have an inherent knack for being brave—to the point of making foolish decisions. But no one had asked me to teach a child to be brave before. All three of them, I thought, my own children and the young prince, were my best chance to make amends for abandoning my own family.

Despite these pains, life was happy. Another year went by in a blink. I no longer worried I was one mistake away from prison or death. There were the joys of libraries and long walks in the garden and the relaxed nature of court life in Arindora. Fersa and I played with the babes and put them to bed and then...we played a bit with each other, shall we say. Fersa paid a visit to Pennarick every few months but she was terrible about writing letters, even if I let her dictate to me. My wife still could barely read but she was learning to play the lute by ear.

"I don't care what you say, it makes more sense to me," she said defensively.

"I didn't say anything."

Queen Bethany and I had barely worked on that book yet. I think she was writing another romance although she tried to pretend otherwise.

I couldn't help it, though. When the heat came upon me, it wasn't enough that I had a wife. I wanted to run with her, run as wolves. I was drawn to the forest, to the wild land visible outside the towers of Arindora. A vast forest stretched just outside of the city. The forest where my kin had died. I couldn't concentrate on anything; I could only stare out at the trees.

Fersa found me there. "My poor caged wolf."

"I want to ask for forgiveness."

"You want to go there?"

I took her hand. "Will you go with me?"

"And leave the children? What if the forest *doesn't* forgive you?"

"To this day, we have never run together as wolves."

Her eyes glinted. She felt it too; she couldn't resist. We were just as foolish as we ever were. "All right."

FERSA

WE SHIFTED BACK into our naked skin, both at once, while we were locked together. "Agnar, you naughty dog..."

"Ah, Fersa, my naughty little bitch..."

My forearms were buried in the snow now, and I shivered but I was also burning with heat as he mounted me from behind, his cock pumping hard into my pussy, his chest against my back, his arms surrounding mine. He nipped at my shoulder. My hair spilled onto the forest floor.

My inner walls started pulsing with pleasure. "Ahh..."

"You always come first," he said. "How do you manage that?"

"I can't help it...it's because you're so good. You always hit it right—there—yes...yesss..."

"Hmph. Come on, then, get on with it." He gripped one of my breasts, giving it a good squeeze. "You taking that tea the midwife gave you? We don't have room for more kits if we wanted them right now."

"Yes."

"I think I'd still better come in your ass."

"Ooh. So dirty."

"Aye, and you ask for nothing less."

"You could come everywhere as far as I'm concerned. How long has it been since we've been this free to howl out our desires?"

He made a rumbling sound of pleasure against my ear and pulled out of my pussy, only to push his rigid manhood into the tighter hole above it. His cock was so slick with all my cum. I groaned, my arousal quickly stirring again as he claimed me there. There was nothing I loved more than for my mate to sate himself in my body, no greater pleasure than to feel his seed filling me up. I felt very awkward talking to the elven women because many of them didn't take the same view of physical pleasures. They were nice enough too, but I still think I occasionally said something that made me sound more like an animal than a girl.

Well, it just couldn't be helped.

"No pinecones on your head yet," I said. "Perhaps your apology was accepted?"

"I don't know if I dare to hope. I didn't know what to say." He frowned. "I'll never know what to say, Fersa. How do you speak to a forest?"

"You told the truth. I suppose that's all you can do." I smiled faintly, thinking of all the truths I'd had to tell. In the end, Father and I were closer after I told him I wanted to marry Agnar, even though he was upset at first. Patrick was right. It was better to tell the truth.

We found our clothes—after a brief moment of horror that we had lost track of them—and dared to take a walk a little deeper in, until we reached the banks of a stream.

Agnar let go of my hand and ran to the bank. He suddenly threw off his pants and shirt—so fast he ripped the buttons off, even though he was trying to save the clothes—turned into a wolf and sniffed the air.

I started pulling off my own dress, worried that he had seen or heard a danger. "What's wrong?"

He changed back, his head slumped toward the icy waters. "I thought—I thought I caught Ergar and Garrin's scent."

"Oh..." I dropped down next to him, urging him away from the water. I didn't want him catching cold.

"I know that's impossible. But it was so strong...for a moment. The forest bears the memories of ghosts."

"Maybe it isn't *just* a ghost...look!"

He lifted his head.

On the opposite bank, through the trees, the form of a blue stag stood before us, although no one had seen one close to the city in many years—its fur a striking color of soft bluish gray, its great horns a polished black. The great guardian of the forest inclined his head. And for a moment, I caught a scent on the wind myself, the scent of the only person so dear to me that I still could hardly bear her loss. I understood. The forest was giving us a gift.

"Agnar...I think you are forgiven."

THANK YOU FOR READING! To make sure you don't miss a release, sign up for my mailing list, and come chat with me on Facebook or drop me a line on Facebook or at lidiyafox-glove@lidiyafoxglove.com! My first original fantasy, a reverse harem trilogy starting with Priestess Awakened, is also out now! If you like romantic fantasy anime or manga you should definitely read it, and if you don't, forget I said that and definitely read it anyway. *eyes fill with dewy hopefulness* But I'm not done with fairy tales either, no...

More Romantic Fantasy from Lidiya!

Fairy Tale Heat

Every book is standalone and can be read in any order, although some characters might pop up in later books!

Book One: Beauty and the Goblin King

Book Two: These Wicked Revels (A retelling of The Twelve Dancing Princesses)

Book Three: Rapunzel and the Dark Prince

Book Four: The Beggar Princess (A retelling of King Thrushbeard)

Book Five: The Goblin Cinderella

Book Six: The Mermaid Bride

Book Seven: Tasting Gretel

Book Eight: Taming Red Riding Hood

Guardians of Sky and Shadow

Book One: Priestess Awakened

Book Two: Priestess Bound

Book Three: Priestess Unleashed

Paranormal Romance

Tempted by Demons

About the Author

Lidiya Foxglove has always loved a good fairy tale, whether it's sweet or steamy, and she likes to throw in a little of both. Sometimes she thinks she ought to do something other than reading and writing, but that would require doing more laundry. So...never mind.

lidiyafoxglove@lidiyafoxglove.com

Made in the USA
Las Vegas, NV
18 February 2022

44190159R00090